Renegades of the Lost Sea

Book Three
Saga of the Outer Islands

A. F. Stewart

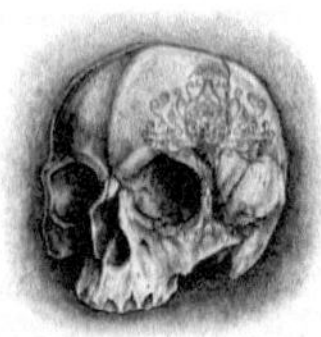

More Books by A. F. Stewart

Multi-Author Anthologies:

Abandon: 13 Tales of Impulse, Betrayal, Surrender, and Withdrawal
A Twist of Fate: A Collection of 11 Twisted Fairy Tales
Beyond the Wail
Legends and Lore
Mechanized Masterpieces
Christmas Lites Series (Books III-VII)
Coffin Hop: Death by Drive-In

Fiction:

Ghosts of the Sea Moon (Saga of the Outer Islands Book I)
Souls of the Dark Sea (Saga of the Outer Islands Book II)
Chronicles of the Undead
Killers and Demons II: They Return
Killers and Demons
Fairy Tale Fusion
Gothic Cavalcade
Ruined City
Once Upon a Dark and Eerie...
Passing Fancies

Poetry:

Primal Elements: An OWS Ink Poetry Anthology
Horror Haiku Pas de Deux
Horror Haiku and Other Poems

Colours of Poetry
Reflections of Poetry
Shadows of Poetry
Tears of Poetry

For all the scallywags.

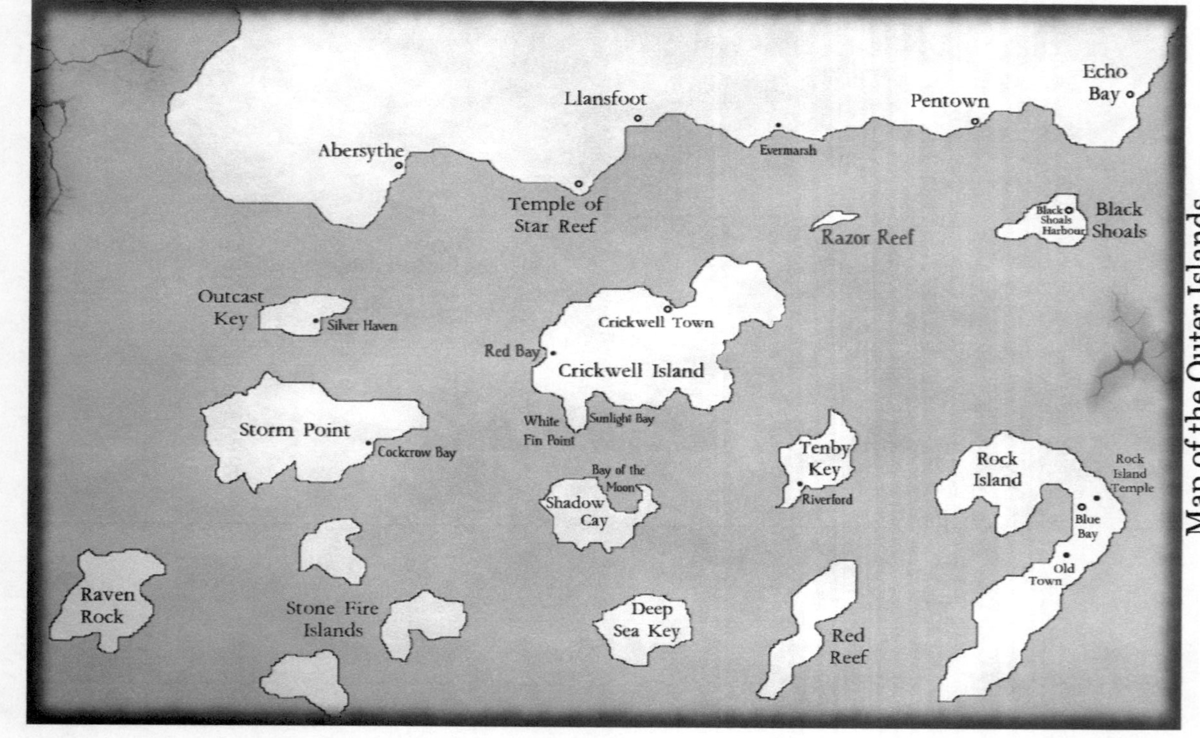

Map of the Outer Islands

Map of the Wakeford Islands Area

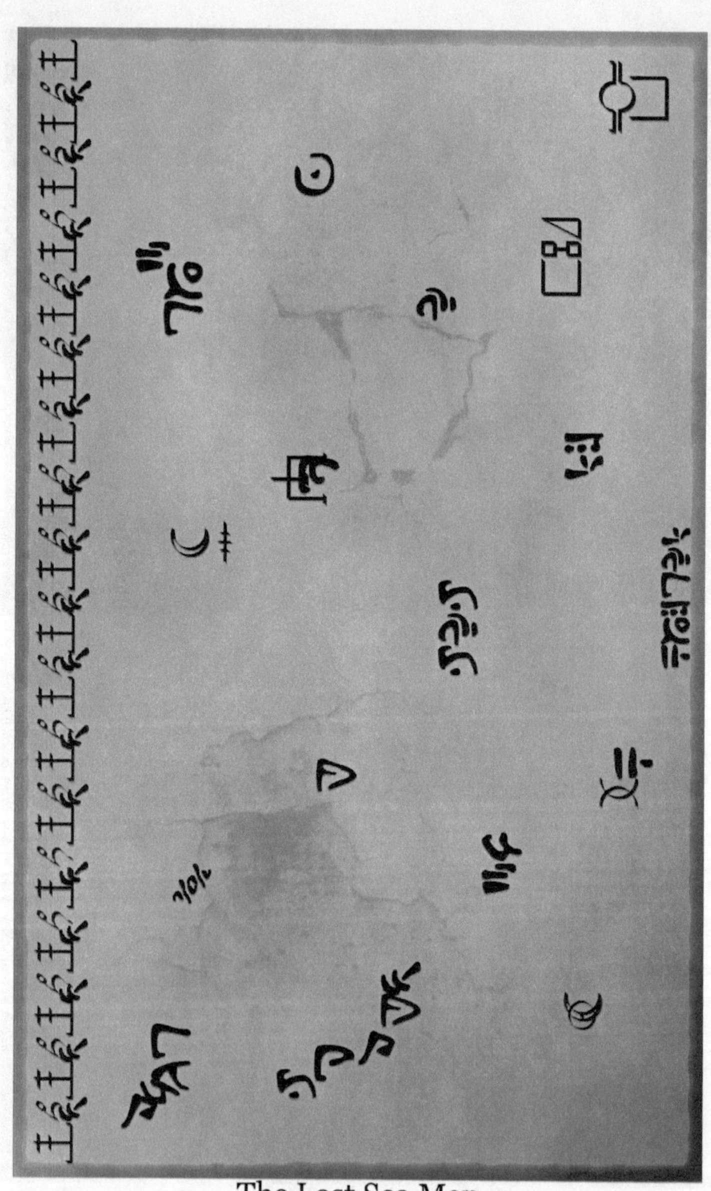

The Lost Sea Map

Contents

Prologue

The moon glimmered in the night sky and a dark-haired child smiled at his sister's light. Snuggled in his warm bed, he stared past his open window at the glowing orb in the sky, until a shadow crossed its radiance. With fascination, the boy watched a black crow manoeuvre across the sky and swoop in for a landing on the windowsill.

The creature settled his wings and cawed a greeting. "Hello, Morrannan."

The boy blinked and inhaled his surprise. Then he smiled, delighted at the prospect of a new friend. He sat up, ready to reply, but the heavy sound of footsteps forestalled him.

"Shadow Bird!" a voice barked out from the bedchamber doorway, and Reis, Sovereign of the Gods, walked into the room. "What are you doing here? If Death finds you here... You know she barred you from the Isle of Shadows and the After World."

"I am pleased you remember, but do not call me Shadow Bird. That part of me died long ago. Ulerne saw to that." Bitterness hung on the words and the bird shifted position, glancing at the sky. "I am the Nightmare Crow now." The Crow cawed, brief and harsh. "As for the banishment... Well, his sister let me in." The Crow nodded at the boy in the bed. "On her moonbeams."

"Manume?" Reis curled his fingers into fists. "What have you done to her?" Beside Reis the boy gasped, fear and confusion in his expression.

"Nothing. I merely had a chat with her. I thought she might prove useful in helping me open the Gateway. To go back to the stars."

"A child! You thought to use a child?"

"Child she may be, but still a goddess." The Crow ruffled his wings. "But do not stress your fatherly worries. She cannot help. She only slips between the edges of realms. She has not the power to open the Gateway." The Crow turned his head slightly. "But you know that. You also know who does. Your son." The Crow bobbed his head at the boy who stared wide-eyed, mouth agape.

Reis took a step forward, putting himself between his son and the Crow. "You are correct, little crow. My son is the key to many things. I think we both know what he can truly do." Reis nodded at the boy. "But that time has not come yet. So fly from this place, on those moonbeams you travelled, and never return."

The Crow flapped his wings. "I'll go. I have what I need. This isn't over though. I have patience. I will wait." The bird leapt from the windowsill and flew away, along the moonlight.

"What just happened, Father?" The boy sat open-mouthed on the bed, his face bewildered. "Did the bird want me to take him to the stars? I can, you know. If you want me to help him. I see them sometimes, the stars, in my dreams."

"Do you now?" Reis smiled, a sad touch to his lips.

"They're beautiful, aren't they?"

The child nodded. "Do you want me to help the bird? I think I can open the door and let him through. I feel it there. I feel all the in-between doors."

"You don't even need the Gateway, do you?" Reis sighed.

His son frowned. "I don't understand."

"No matter. All I meant is your magic is so very strong. Strong enough to remake the world." Reis walked over and sat on the bed, tousling his son's hair.

The boy giggled. Then he lowered his eyes, making circles on the bedcovers with a finger. "Father, are the worlds broken?"

Reis' heart skipped a beat. "Why do you ask?"

The boy looked up, a strange expression in his eyes. "Sometimes I sneak through the in-between doors and go wandering. When I go certain places, things feel wrong. Are they wrong?"

Reis hesitated, but then replied, "Yes."

The boy gave a sigh. "Do you want me to fix it? I can, and make everyone happy again. Even that crow."

"No, son," Reis smiled. "It is not time yet for you to fix things. And don't worry about that bird. I'll take care of him. The Crow is old family business. He won't bother you anymore."

"I don't know. He seemed...determined." The boy struggled with the last word as if unsure he expressed himself correctly. "And the worlds..."

Reis shook his head. "Not for you to worry about. Perhaps someday, but for today, everything is fine. And it is time for bed." Reis nodded at the pillow and his son settled back down. Reis stroked his head, smoothing some errant strands off the child's forehead. "Someday you'll understand, Morrannan. Now go back to your slumber and forget."

Silver magic sparked under Reis' fingers, an energy that penetrated its way deep into the boy's mind, power weaving into memory.

Reis whispered, "*Lluich serei angaofi,*" and the night's events faded from his son's mind. With two more words, "*Athgofin anghywyr,*" his magic gathered certain bits of his son's thoughts and knowledge, and all recollection of the realms' in-between doors. It collected the child's memories behind barriers and partitions as the space where they existed settled into dreams and dust. Soon nothing of these things remained accessible in the boy's psyche. Morrannan closed his eyes, suddenly exhausted.

Reis smiled, a gesture of regret and bitter acceptance, as he withdrew the magic from his child. "Now go to sleep, my little God of Souls. And forget all about crows."

A father watched his son fall asleep with a sigh and a final whisper.

"You are better off not knowing what you are yet. Better off forgetting it all. I only hope you can forgive me."

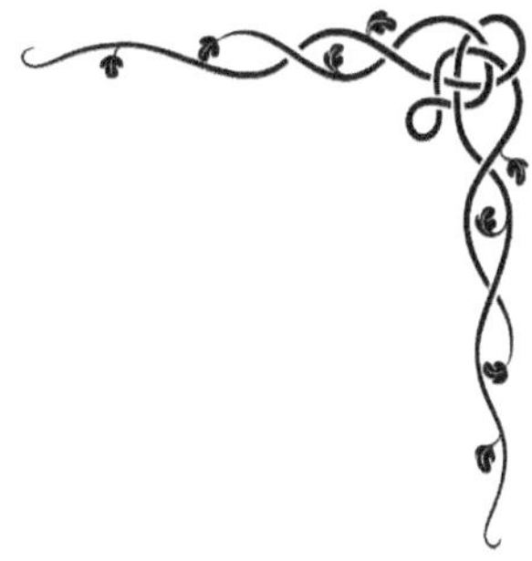

Chapter One
Meetings

Beneath a warm sun, on a bright afternoon, the ocean waves gently rocked along their flowing currents, swirling around the Outer Islands. Among the clouds, a black silhouette flitted; a bird, the Nightmare Crow. He soared through the blue sky, this perfect day, headed south, past Shadow Cay and onward, the hours turning to days and ticking by with the beat of his wings.

He went beyond the Wakeford Islands, ascending over their fields of tea and farmland, and farther still. As sunset turned to starlight, he reached the Great Southern Mists. There, he wheeled in flight, skirting the outside of the fog, dipping and veering among the grey vapours. His voice whispered, on the tide of air, words given him years ago by a reckless man of magic. The haze opened him a path, granting him access beyond the barrier. He crossed the mists and flew past the Edge of the World, continuing his journey until he reached the vast expanse of ocean called the Lost Sea.

There, the sea swelled in light waves, their colour reflecting, to his gaze, a darker hue than the seas of the Outer Islands. The water tossed as a sickly green with red undertones, the tint reflected from a strange-coloured sky. Any vibrant blues and warm sun had vanished, replaced with a pale mauve against red-grey clouds and washed out light. A shiver ran along the Crow's feathers, as memories of a former life and of finding this place danced in his head, but he pushed onward.

He flew unerringly above the water, heading for an uninhabited and unnamed island known only to a few across centuries. For eons he searched for it, travelled the dream corridors time and again, rebuffed by magic and men who served his enemies. Until one answered his call many years ago. A curious soul, dissatisfied and restless, open to his influence, who showed him the way.

The Crow smiled, remembering that day—the moment he found the island, saw once again the Gateway of the Realms. From there he cultivated a partnership with its guardian, the magic user who called himself a necromancer. Now he came to reap the fruits of that decades-old alliance, and see the culmination of his schemes.

Upon spotting the island, the Crow descended through the sky, skimming the treetops, making his way towards the only visible structure on the isle: a stone temple. He settled on its rooftop and let out a loud caw. His greeting was met with silence. The Crow ruffled his feathers and cawed again, even louder. Again no answer came, only silence.

Angered, the Crow lifted his wings and leapt from the roof, gliding down to the courtyard below. "Show yourself, necromancer! I demand an audience!"

"And who be making demands at my front door?" a voice unfamiliar to the Crow answered, and the temple door creaked open. In the doorway stood a gaunt, pale man with black hair and a scraggly beard, dressed in the ragged clothes of a sea captain. He looked down at the Crow. "A black bird, is it? Odd. Where's the impudent fellow who demanded to see my former jailor?"

"I'm right here." The Crow lifted his head as he spoke and then clacked his beak.

The man smiled, without menace yet somehow a touch sinister. "A bird that talks, are ye? Do you have a name?"

"I am called the Nightmare Crow."

"Are ye now? That's quite the moniker. I'm Black Axe Morgan." He widened his smile, the sinister creeping across his face. "And this be my island, at present. You be trespassing, so state your business, please."

"Your island?" The Crow took a step back, surprised, and flapped his wings. "What happened to the necromancer?"

"Oh, he's still around." Black Axe Morgan chuckled. "Just not as lively as he used to be." He leaned forward and whispered, "Want to see him, Mr. Nightmare Crow?"

The Crow drew his wings to his body, wary, but replied, "Yes."

"Follow me, then." Morgan walked back inside the temple and the Crow chased after him, fluttering up the steps and then walking through the open doorway. Morgan stopped at a cabinet at the far end of the temple antechamber and the Crow flew to a nearby table. "So where is..." The words trailed off, as he saw the gleaming white skull sitting behind the glass cabinet door.

"There be the head of the necromancer, the gods rot his wicked soul." Morgan laughed. "The bastard got what he deserved. Never saw it coming. Never thought I'd do it."

"Do what exactly?" the Crow asked slowly, unsure of who or what he was dealing with now.

"Kill him, of course. And steal his dark magic while I

was at it. There ain't no necromancer no more. Only me." Morgan turned to the Crow tilting his head. He held out a hand and spoke one word, "*Ffamlau.*" Green energy, much like fire, formed around his hand.

"Well now, that is an interesting turn of events." The Crow relaxed, yet stared at Black Axe Morgan. "The name sounds familiar. You were a pirate, is that right?"

"Aye, I was." The man scowled.

"A man with a dark heart, I like that." The Crow chuckled. "And one to reckon with as well. I've never heard of anyone stealing a necromancer's magic before. How did you manage it?"

"We were connected, he and I. Made things simple in the end."

The Crow moved a step closer to the man. "Connected? How?"

"He used his cursed magic to resurrect me from the dead. The bloody stuff ran through my veins." Morgan spat. "He said I was his great achievement and kept me around as his bloody trophy. He shouldn'ta done that, though, 'cause I learned things." Morgan shrugged. "But all you really need to know is I control it now, his magic." He grinned. "Is that what you come for, bird? One of his tricks? 'Cause if it is, you need to parley with me now."

"I have no issue with that. I see no reason you and I cannot reach an accord similar to what I had with the necromancer." The Crow stretched out his wings. "What do you want, Mr. Black Axe Morgan?"

"I want my life back!" The words were snarled, like a savage beast snapping at its prey. "I want what was stolen from me and I want revenge on that bastard Rafe Morrow!"

The Crow flapped his wings, surprised. Then he laughed. "Oh, Morgan, I very much think we can help each other. I very much do."

Rafe Morrow stood in the middle of the tavern, a mug of ale in his hand, surrounded by men shouting, "Drink, drink, drink!" The captain brandished the ale and downed the entire mug without stopping or taking a breath. Then he held the empty mug above his head in triumph as a roar of glee surged from the crowd. Rafe thumped the mug on the table in front of him and cried, "Another!"

Slumped at the table, his opponent in the drinking game lifted his head and his glass of ale, only to smile and pass out, spilling the ale and sprawling on the tavern floor. Rafe lifted his now refilled mug, exclaiming, "To Jervis, a fine sailor who can't hold his liquor!" before draining yet another draught of fine ale. A further chorus of cheers followed and more than a few sailors drained ale down their throats to celebrate the captain's victory.

Rafe put the again empty mug on the table and wandered back, with a slightly unsteady gait, to sit with his crewmates, cheerfully accepting the back slaps and congratulations as he strolled. He sat down with a smile. Blackthorne matched his smile.

"Well, that was a show, sir." Beside him Short Davy nodded in agreement while he chewed a large helping of greasy meat pie

"Aye," One-Eyed Anders chimed in, "and a mighty fine one, sir." He glanced over his shoulder at the man who had passed out on the floor, now being carried out of the tavern by his friends. "Serves the fool right for thinking he could out-drink our captain."

Rafe chuckled. "I did warn him. It was good fun though."

"And it caught us a little coin." Anders grinned and clicked the money purse at his belt. "One or two men were willing to bet against you, sir. To their shame." He nodded his head at a table of dejected fellows nursing their ale.

"Anders. I'm shocked." Rafe grinned, countering his words. "Only one or two? Last time you managed to talk at least four into wagering."

As the men laughed, footsteps approached, and a shadow fell over the table. "Morrannan. Listen to me."

Rafe looked up in shock at hearing his given godly name, expecting one of his family to be standing there. Instead, a scruffy sailor stood by the table, her eyes reflecting a shade of coal-black. She spoke again.

"The endgame is here. The Crow is coming. You must prepare for the final battle."

Then the black in the woman's eyes faded to a normal blue, and she looked around, confused. "What am I doing here? I was on my ship, I was…" She stopped speaking and stared at Rafe.

"It's all right, lass," the captain replied in a soothing voice. "Go back to your ship. You did what you needed to do, and it's over."

She nodded and hurried off as if chased by a sea monster.

The silence at the table was broken by Blackthorne. "What was that all about, sir?"

"A warning. Trouble's coming, boys."

Chapter Two
Pirates

Black Axe Morgan stared at the Nightmare Crow, glaring the same ugly sneering look he'd fixed on his face and held for the last ten minutes. The Crow tilted his head with amusement and finally broke the silent stalemate.

"So you're one of them, are you? One of his subjects, his resurrected dead?"

"Aye." The word seemed pulled out of Morgan as if the admittance was distasteful. "He brought me back, the bastard. I thought I was saved, I did, when he yanked my soul in, away from wandering the world. Didn't know I'd end up his slave." Morgan spat on the floor to emphasize his disgust. "But I turned the tables, yes I did."

"Well, good for you. I never much liked that overbearing sorcerer. He was useful, but I think you may be more useful." The Crow chuckled. "Tell me more about your resurrection. I find that interesting. I didn't know the necromancer perfected his abilities in that area. I witnessed some of his earlier failures. Most nasty. Are you the only success?"

Morgan laughed, deep and harsh. "Not at all. The bastard was busy before I killed him. Would you like to see them all, Mr. Nightmare Crow?"

The Crow stretched his wings. "Indeed I would."

The Crow watched Black Axe Morgan descend a stairway leading beneath the temple until he was swallowed by the darkness below. He did not relish the thought of flying into the pitch-black unknown, so the creature half-flew, half-hopped down the steps, slowly following where the other man led.

"Hurry it up, bird!" an impatient shout echoed back from the underground depths.

The Crow clacked his beak and answered, "I'm coming as fast as I can!" He ruffled his feathers with an angry caw and heard clumping footsteps approaching. Black Axe Morgan came back into view.

"Aye, that's a problem. Birds ain't made for stair climbing." He reached over and scooped up the Crow, who cawed in protest. "Shut your beak. It'll be faster if I carry ye." Perturbed at the indignity, the Crow nonetheless allowed the man to tuck him under an arm and walk them both down the long staircase and into dark tunnels beneath the temple.

At the bottom, Morgan put his hand on a stone wall, and breathed out another spell word, *"Efenglauge."* A line of deep green flickering energy snaked along the wall and down the tunnel, lighting the place in a dim emerald light.

The Crow remarked, "Interesting. You're an adept spell worker. Did the necromancer teach you his tricks before you killed him?"

Morgan grunted. "Yeah, I'm full of tricks these days. And he did teach me some, like he was training a dog, but mostly I watched him as he worked and learned things, like I said before. The rest of the skill, well, it seemed to come with the magic when I stole it."

"Really?" A note of curiosity crept into the Crow's voice. "How exactly did you steal his magic?"

"Wouldn't you like to know?" Morgan chuckled. "So you can take it for yourself, I'm betting. I ain't stupid, Mr. Nightmare Crow."

The Crow squirmed as Morgan's grip tightened slightly, replying, "Of course not. I never meant to imply any insult." He poked his beak at Morgan's hand, and the grip loosened. "And you're welcome to keep your magic. If I wanted it, I would have taken it already. I'm just curious about your method."

Morgan grunted. "Maybe. Maybe not. We'll see about telling secrets later." Morgan stopped walking. "We've arrived." He leaned over and put the Crow down on the floor. "Here they be, the not-so-dead of this forsaken island, the poor wretches enslaved by the necromancer and his unnatural magic." Morgan extended his arm in a grand sweeping motion, trailing green light from his fingers. The illumination revealed a wide cavern: catacombs full of carved niches in the walls. Dozens of bodies filled the stone tombs.

The Crow gaped, disappointment seeping into his bones. "They're all dead?"

"Nah. Each one of those poor fools is alive. Leastwise been resurrected from the dead. They're just sleeping. The necromancer bastard put a spell on them or something."

"Fascinating." The Crow peered along the rows. "How did he manage to find so many?"

"Shipwrecks mostly, off Outlaw Keys and the Wakeford Islands. Them monsters don't come south much, so I guess he was able to snag uncrossed souls and their corpses easy enough." Morgan spat, the spittle seeping between the cracks in the stone floor. "Most of them wretches he got from a skirmish twixt the navy and some disreputable smugglers. Three ships went down that day, I think. Didn't get them all at once though, so some got a touch of rot or had bits missing before he stopped the decay."

"You seem in good shape." The Crow glanced at Morgan.

"Aye. He must have snagged my body up quick. Sure as spit took his time with my soul though. The bastard." Morgan scowled.

"My sympathies." The Crow twitched his feathers and turned his attention back to the catacombs. "I want a closer look."

The Crow took a few steps forward, craning his head to get a better look at the still occupants of the tombs. He could see wisps of green and grey energy and felt the magic drift out from the walls. The Crow chuckled. "You always did like the old tricks, didn't you?"

"What are you jabbering about?" Morgan demanded from behind him. "You know something, bird?"

"Indeed, I do. I know how to wake these souls." He turned to Black Axe Morgan, asking, "How would you like to wage a war, sir?"

"Maybe I would, maybe I wouldn't." Morgan tilted his head with a smile. "Depends on who I be warring against."

"Captain Rafe Morrow, of course."

Morgan snarled. "Why didn't you say so from the beginning! Let's raise them bastards and go to war!"

Sitting on the beach, her eyes closed and basking in her moonlight, Manume held a bleached white skull and listened for its voice in the still of the night. She heard nothing, not a whisper, not a shout, not a single word.

She opened her eyes and placed the skull on the sand, staring. "Why won't you talk to me? You invited me. You said come. Silly skull. Playing tricks." She frowned. "I don't like tricks."

Black wisps curled out of the skull, a wreath of haze dancing around the bone. A voice echoed against the sound of the sea and wind. "No tricks, daughter. It just takes time to travel to your world. My apologies for the delay."

Manume tilted her head. "Mother? Come for a visit? Interesting."

"These are interesting times. And much to do."

"To do? To do? Are you setting me some tasks, Mother dear? To spread my moonbeams and sew together the world you broke?" Her voice held a lilt of amusement, but underneath came a strain of resentment. "Am I to clean another mess you made? Isn't dispatching a monstrous brother enough?"

"So you knew." The disembodied voice seemed to sigh. "How?"

The Moon Goddess shrugged. "The bones talk. More than willing to spill your secrets."

There was a moment of silence and then, "Did they tell you about the Crow?"

Manume scowled. "Enough, I think. Didn't want to know more. Nasty bird. Didn't want to know about bird and Mother." She flicked sand at the skull.

Another ethereal sigh. "I'm sorry. This shouldn't be your problem. My mistakes should not be your burden."

"But they are. The Crow made it so." Manume curled her arms around her knees. "But I understand mistakes. Made my own." She danced a sliver of moonlight along her skin, chasing the tattoos her brother had etched with his magic. "What do you need me to do, Mother?"

"Help me stop the Crow. Help me save your brother. Help me save the worlds."

Chapter Three
Gifts

The sails of the *Celestial Jewel* billowed in the prevailing wind, and she cut through the waves doing a fast clip, headed to Rock Island Temple. Rafe stood at the rail of the quarterdeck, watching the sunlight sparkle off the water, but his mood was anything but happy. Elliot Blackthorne hovered behind him.

"It seems you were right, Blackthorne."

The first mate eased in beside Rafe at the rail, looking first at his captain and then at the beautiful day. "Right about what, sir?"

"About the Crow not being done with us."

"Aye, sir. An endgame, she said. That sounds more personal than the previous times, doesn't it? Like he's finally ready to show himself."

"That's what worries me. A final gambit, winner take all." Rafe glanced at Blackthorne before he turned back to stare at the sea. "Do we even know the stakes? Or the rules? How do you defeat an opponent if you don't know the game?"

"Maybe by doing what we do best, sir. Improvise and take things as they come, with a sword in our hand and the wind at our back."

Rafe chuckled. "We are good at that."

Blackthorne leaned against the rail. "I say let this Crow come, show himself at last. I'm tired of fighting shadows and I'd lay the odds in our favour any day."

Rafe smiled despite his mood. "No more baleful predictions?"

"No, sir." Blackthorne shifted his feet. "I have been a bit sour of late, but that's done. Bring whatever is coming, I say. It's past time for a reckoning."

"On that we agree. This Crow needs to be dealt with."

"Aye, he does. Head on and full sails." Blackthorne pushed off from the rail and straightened his spine. "And whatever happens, the crew is with you, sir, as always."

"I know that, but thank you for the reminder. Let's hope the Oracle can help us with that fight."

Blackthorne nodded and a comfortable silence fell between them, the sun shining bright and the waves slapping against the ship. Momentum rumbled under their feet and the *Jewel* picked up speed.

The Oracle was waiting for Rafe when he entered her chambers. The young girl smiled at him from her high-backed chair, swinging her legs and swishing her skirts. A tea service sat on a table in front of her, swirls of steam wafting out from the pot. She already held a cup.

"Hello, God of Souls. I was expecting you so I had some tea brought in. Please, have a cup."

Rafe nodded politely, trying not to show his surprise or irritation. Lately, too many people knew more about his own life than he did, it seemed. He crossed the room, sat down on a chair and poured himself a cup of tea. Sipping, he asked, "A blend from Idria?"

The Oracle smiled. "Yes. My mother favoured their teas. Her one indulgence. But you haven't come to chat about tea." She leaned over and put her cup down on the table. "You've come to talk about the Crow."

Rafe leaned back in his chair. This child was far more direct than Amaratha. He still found it disconcerting, but it matched her forthright demeanour. "I am. What do you know?"

"That you are both destined to meet at last. All the paths of fate have merged into one. Old enemies, past sins—it all brings us here." She sighed, a gentle sound full of sadness and hope.

Rafe matched her sigh. "Anything more specific?"

"That is her tale, and the tale of others." The Oracle nodded, her gaze directed behind Rafe. He turned to see the Goddess of the Moon walk across the room.

She stopped a foot away from her brother, her blue cloak trailing on the marble floor, and tilted her head. "Hello. Mother sent me."

Rafe sucked in a breath and gripped the arm of his chair. "Mother?"

Manume nodded. "Talked to me through a skull. Told me things. Gave me things."

Rafe calmed his breathing, feeling his heart thump. "Mother is involved in this?"

"I know. Most strange." His sister crinkled her nose and shrugged. "She wanted you to have these." She reached into a bag slung over her shoulder and withdrew two items: a book and a roll of parchment. She held out the parchment to Rafe. "This is a map."

Rafe gingerly took the offered document, biting back all his questions, and unrolled the chart. Confusion bloomed across his face. "What is this? It's all odd markings and symbols. There are no landmarks, no sea lanes."

The Goddess of the Moon tilted her head. "Mother said something about navigating a Lost Sea. I wasn't paying much attention." She sniffed. "Besides it all looked like squiggles to me."

Rafe inhaled sharply. "Navigating the Lost Sea? Are you sure? That's never been done! No one has been able to sail farther south than the Outlaw Keys."

"Oh. That place. I've heard of that. Great mists and hidden things." She shrugged again. "Could be. Could be that map. Wouldn't know. I never travelled there before."

"I did once, with Harley." The words drifted out, an unbidden memory. "We sailed past the Wakeford Islands, after a cargo run, and tried to chart the Great Southern Mists." A smile crossed Rafe's face. "It didn't go well."

"Who's Harley?" The goddess' voice broke against Rafe's musings.

"What?" For a moment Rafe looked bewildered, then added, "Just an old friend. From many years ago."

"Dead then." Manume sniffed. "More bones. Mother said you would need the map later, but also this." She held out the book. "Secrets of sorcerers and schemes, and something called a necromancer. Didn't sound nice. He dabbled in dead things."

Rafe twitched a grin and accepted the book from his sister. "I'm familiar with necromancy. That practice of magic was outlawed years ago." He ran a finger over the worn leather cover before flipping through the pages. "It's a journal?"

"Several, I think. All in one book." The Moon Goddess scuffed her foot. "Jibber jabber if you ask me, but Mother said it would help."

"You read it?" Rafe closed the book and looked up at

his sister.

"Some of it. Some not. Mostly the last bits. I got bored." She giggled. "Spells and ego, what I read. Mortal prattling. And silliness about the dead. Don't think this necromancer knew much. Didn't want to let the dead stay dead. Don't know why. Not good company, the dead."

Rafe smiled. "I can't agree. I find the souls of the dead make excellent company."

Manume wrinkled her nose. "You deal with *souls*. He yammered on about bones and bodies. Not the same. Bones talk too much about nothing. But you'll see."

"I suppose I will." Rafe tucked the book and map into his coat pocket. "Did Mother say anything else?"

"Only that she's coming to visit you." Manume chuckled at Rafe's shock. "I know. Wish I could see it, but I have things to do. Things to do. Mother has some errands for me." She smiled. "She wants you to do something too. Sail south."

The Goddess of the Moon laughed and glided out of the room, headed only she knew where. She left Rafe staring at the wall filled with dread at the thought of his mother's visit.

She walked the long path through her realm, stirring the dust of ages and the broken dead. Cold air travelled with her, zephyrs dragged from the bottomless depths of infinite darkness. Stale air from before the Light, before the stars, a touch of the breath of Chaos herself.

Shadows fell away as she passed, moaning things that scurried far from her footsteps lest she see them and be displeased. She moved in silence as all the shrieks and whimpers—the discordant rhythm of her home—ceased in the wake of her journey.

Yet, she paid none of it any heed. She thought only

of her destination. For the first time in centuries, she returned to the world of mortal beings.

Death was coming into the Light.

Chapter Four
Expectations

"Did you bring the rum, Blackthorne?"

The first mate grinned, holding up the bottle, and closed the door to the captain's quarters. "A bottle of Sun Rock from Storm Point, sir."

Rafe matched Blackthorne's grin. "An excellent choice." He pushed two glasses forward on his desk. "Pour us both a dram. Then we will discuss this." He tapped the leather-bound journal, also sitting on his desk.

"Aye, sir." Blackthorne opened the bottle and poured a generous amount of rum into two glasses. The fragrant aroma of the spiced liquor drifted into the air as he closed the bottle and set it aside. Blackthorne picked up his glass and settled in a chair. He looked at his captain expectantly.

Rafe reached across his desk and lifted the other glass, taking a sip before speaking. "I don't know what to make of it all. Being handed maps and journals and..." He took another hasty sip of rum. "My mother coming."

"Aye. That is a development." Blackthorne drank

some of his rum. "One I don't like to think on. But at least we have something to do in the meantime. The ship's headed south, towards the Wakeford Islands, and Anders is studying that map you got from your sister. He hasn't had much luck with it so far." He paused, glancing at the journal. "Did you read that thing yet?" He nodded at the book. "Or have you simply been staring at it."

Rafe chuckled. "I've opened it, skimmed through it and read a bit of the beginning. The damn thing seems to have been written by several people. Guardians of some sort, and from what I gathered, members of the Society of the Shadow Guard."

"Them again? They're involved in whatever's going on?"

"Aye, they are. Or were. I'm not sure how this journal fits in to the trouble that's coming. Or how it all connects to my mother. Or, for that matter, what the dark depths is going on."

"Now, Captain, when do we ever know what's going on? Lately the bloody world seems bent on throwing danger our way and letting us figure things out as we go. And we've done well so far. We're old hands at improvising now, aren't we?"

"Aye. Doesn't make it less frustrating though."

"Nonetheless, it does keep us on our toes." Blackthorne smiled as he took a sip of rum. "What did you find in the book so far? Anything interesting?"

Rafe nodded. "The beginning was written in the Odiki language by an ancient practitioner of magic. From what I've been able to decipher, he was one of the first members of the Society of the Shadow Guard tasked with protecting some island in the Lost Sea. Here, I'll read you a passage." Rafe picked up the journal and flipped open to the first few pages.

"I have sailed far south in this new, strange world at the behest of our gods, to my new home. I have agreed to defend this sacred place against encroachment and dark forces. The power to shield this place has been granted me, and I do so willingly, giving my existence to the service of my gods."

"A bit flowery speech-wise, but straightforward enough. Might be trouble though, if this island is our objective. Sounds like it's protected by magic." Blackthorne smiled at Rafe's quizzical look. "Meaning it won't be easy to find, if that's what we mean to do."

"True, but we may already have the key. Listen." Rafe flipped another few pages. *"It is done. The great veil has been created. An ever-swirling, moving wall of mist to shroud this place from prying eyes."* Rafe closed the journal. "That sounds like the Great Southern Mists to me. So if we can work out the map, finding the island may not be difficult. If indeed that's what we're supposed to be doing."

Blackthorne shrugged and finished the last drop of rum in his glass. "It's as good a plan as any, sir. Given what we have to work with." He reached over and poured himself another glass of rum. "Find anything else of interest in that book?"

"Not yet. The man who penned the first section likes to pontificate about his service to the gods quite a bit, giving them praise and going on about how he's willing to sacrifice to their will. Unfortunately, he doesn't give much detail about his actions or mention which gods he serves. I can see why Manume found reading the journal boring."

"Well, there must be something in it. Why else would your mother send it on to you?"

"Yes. That is the question, isn't it?" Rafe's fingers drummed a nervous beat on his desk. "Why did Mother send me the journal and the map? And where did she obtain it in the first place? Was she one of the gods who wanted this island hidden from the world? And why would it need to be hidden?" Rafe paused for a moment to catch his breath. "And why in all the seas and kingdoms is she leaving her realm to come back to the world of mortals?"

"That's more than one question, sir, and I expect I'm the wrong person to be asking. If your mother is coming, and that is a daunting thing I agree, she's the one you need to question. This may be out of place to be saying, but I think you and she need to have a long talk about things. Especially considering the secrets that have come to light lately."

Rafe sighed. "You are right, Blackthorne, but that is one conversation I would prefer to avoid. My mother is..." Rafe let his words die and downed the remainder of his glass of rum instead.

"Aye, sir." Blackthorne nodded in sympathy. "Mothers are difficult enough without adding gods into the mix. I get tongue-tied with my mum and she's not near as imposing as yours. I couldn't even begin to fathom having that conversation."

Rafe smiled slightly. "She's not much of a conversationalist. Much more of the dark and silent type, my mother. More of a great looming shadow than a nurturing presence." Rafe poured himself another glass of rum. "Still, she did try in her own way. It's not as if she was cold. But you could never quite escape the fact that she was Death."

"Though I expect that kept you all a well-behaved lot. Her presence."

"Now I wouldn't go that far." Rafe grinned. "We got into a few scrapes growing up." Then his face clouded. "Still, the thought of talking to her makes me want to turn tail and flee." He chuckled softly, somehow mixed with a sigh. "Isn't that ridiculous? A centuries-old god afraid of his mother?"

Blackthorne grinned slightly. "Not considering *your* mother. I mean, crewing on this ship I've seen a fair bit, but talking with Death herself." He shook his head. "Enough to make the blood run cold. But the fact she's even coming… well that says it all, I think. About the serious nature of what we're facing."

Rafe nodded. "In that, you are correct. Whatever my personal trepidation, I will have to meet with her and find out what the damnation is going on."

"Aye to that, sir." Blackthorne raised his glass and Rafe matched his salute. They both drank their rum and silently shivered at the thought of the future.

The Nightmare Crow perched on a stone ledge in the necromancer's catacombs. Soft wisps of black shadow drifted from his feathers. Tiny threads of magic wafted on the air, floating quietly to each sleeper and burrowing into their heads. The skin of each resurrected body glowed a faint green as the necromancer's magic reacted with the Crow's.

The Crow gave a soft caw and shuttered his eyes. In a sing-song voice he intoned, "Come to me in dreams. *Veltoac etva.* Rise from your slumber. *Veltoac etva.*"

With the words, the bodies twitched and faint moans echoed in the tunnels. The green glow of their skin faded to grey and then changed to translucent black. The twitching ceased, and the Crow clacked his beak.

"It's done. They'll awaken in a few hours."

"And what good will it do?" Black Axe Morgan walked forward from the shadows. "We're stuck here, no way off the island. 'Cept you, of course, but you ain't flying us all away from here. We got no ships. Mine sure as all damnation is at the bottom of the sea, thanks to Captain Morrow." Morgan scowled. "She was a good ship, too, the *Dark Ravager*."

"Oh, you can escape well enough. And I'm sure you lot can steal new ships once you're free."

Morgan snorted. "How do ya propose we escape? Walk across the sea? Or are you going to make us sprout wings so we can fly away?"

The Crow chuckled. "Nothing quite so outlandish. We'll use the great secret of this place, sir. The reason I came. The Gateway."

"The what?" Morgan looked confused.

The Crow fluttered his wings and chuckled again. "You'll see."

Chapter Five
Revelations and Messages

Rafe reclined in his bunk and picked up the journal. Lamplight illuminated the pages as he opened the book, and only the gentle lap of the sea broke the quiet of his chambers.

He flipped past the section he'd already read and skimmed here and there through more of the writings until he reached the end. The last entry, written by the necromancer his sister mentioned, was only a few pages long. Rafe leaned back against his pillows and read.

It didn't work again! It must have been the blood. Not strong enough. Or the bones were too old. I got the spell right. I did! The connection held for a minute, I talked to the spirit. It just wasn't strong enough. Damn this place! I know I can't do my work anywhere else, but it's too remote. Too isolated. Too far away from the dead. I never should have come. But I didn't have much choice. I don't know. It was easier in the beginning. Sometimes I wish I had never angered him that I could still leave this place. Maybe I went too far, but to limit my power like that... It wasn't fair.

Bemused, Rafe rolled his eyes at the complaints of the sorcerer and his floundering attempts at using his dark magic. "Manume was right, he did write about spells and ego." Rafe chuckled and continued reading.

I had a visitor today, a crow. He said he could make the portal work again if we worked together. I could leave this place. I like that idea.

Rafe sat up and quickly flipped the page. He frowned. The entries stopped, and he turned two more blank pages until he reached the end of the book. Then he noticed an inscription on the inside of the back cover. He ran a finger over the raised lettering and instinctively whispered the word aloud.

"*Ynatgyly.*"

The moment he spoke he knew he had activated a concealment spell, a displacement of one object with another. The journal he held suddenly glowed, shimmering in a silver-white energy, before it dissolved and reformed. When the light faded, Rafe stared at something new. A smaller book, bound in a black leather cover with an inscription etched on the front: For my son, Morrannan.

His hand trembling, he opened it, turning the pages until he saw familiar handwriting. He sucked in a breath.

"*Father.*"

He closed his eyes for a moment, thoughts shifting in his head.

What happened? What's my father to do with all this? Why did he hide his writings inside another book?

His mind awash in unease, but curiosity scratching at him, he opened his eyes and began reading what Reis had written.

I set these words to paper because I cannot rid myself of this aversion I have to my new life here. To these tasks set for me by my father and by Death. I do my duty, but I do not like it. This subterfuge and the secrets I must keep rankle my conscience. Phea likes it even less than I. She keeps distracted with our daughters, but I see it in her eyes, the disgust. And she won't even acknowledge the arranged marriage with Death, nor welcome her as my second wife. She blames my father for all this, and me for not refusing him. I cannot fault her for those feelings.

Rafe paused, suddenly uncomfortable. This unexpected insight into his father's life felt unnerving and a bit ignominious. He hesitated, thinking for a moment to shut the journal and not read on, but he continued.

Death is such an inscrutable creature. So practical and cold, yet sometimes I see such sadness. Perhaps it is the losses she suffered. She has loved, I know that. And now she is alone with strangers. Yet, she continues her work. Continues to protect her world even though it has transformed into something she barely tolerates. I know she goes to the Archipelago to see her old friends, and I will not question her on the matter. I allow her that dignity at least. On this other matter, though, I will need guidance. Transforming the world, I understand. It was the only way to stabilize this realm after Father's interference. But setting ourselves as gods to its people—that I do not like. At least she agreed to our separation, our own home in her new world of spirits, with an island portal back to the mortals if we so choose.

Rafe ran a finger along the pages, tracing his father's handwriting. "So this is what it was like, the creation of the Isle of Shadows, the gods' place in the After World." His whispering voice trembled, tinted with awe and surprise. Then he resumed reading.

And this task of Father's I like even less, this creation of a Society. He says it is to safeguard against the darkness, but I see through these visits of his, these duties he gives me. He wants spies and allies. I know he wishes to take this realm from Death. To claim it for the Realm of the Stars. He thinks he does right bringing the Light to this place, and perhaps he has done some good, but I see the scars he left. I will create this Society for him, but not to aid him. In that, I am resolved. If Death wants gods to reign over this new world, then she will have ones that protect the people. My father does not know I have taken his bow and horn. That will be my first task. To give them to this Society of the Shadow Guard to hide. The next task will be to bar the Gateway so Ulerne the Hunter can never return to this realm.

Rafe inhaled sharply and stared at the page, shock running through his skin. More thoughts tumbled past his lips. "My father hid the horn and bow, not Grandfather? And what gateway? I feel like I should know the answer, as if I..." Rafe frowned, exhaling. "How many secrets are there in my family? How many misdirected stories to hide the truth? Is *this* even true?" He turned the page, wondering what else he would find.

I do not like this deception I practice, this godly

pretence and the subservience of mortals, but it has served a purpose. I found who I needed, a magic practitioner willing to be a guardian and protect the Gateway. I fear there is little time to achieve my plan. Father may return at any moment, and now the Shadow Bird has returned. He wants me to send him home, back to the Realm of the Stars. But my father wants none of him anymore. Such a judgemental man my father has become. So cruel now, in many ways. I sought to repair the rift between the Shadow Bird and Death instead, but it did not go well.

A knock on the door of his quarters broke the quiet and Rafe looked up from the journal, startled by the abrupt noise. Blackthorne's voice followed on the heels of the knocking.

"Captain! We may have trouble. Or a visitor. Or something."

Rafe closed the journal with a snap and tossed it gently on his bunk as he sprang to his feet. Moments later he was across the room and yanked open the door. A pale and haggard-looking Blackthorne stood waiting.

"There's a Sea Ghoul drifting off the starboard side, sir. Not threatening, just following. Don't know what to bloody make of it, sir."

Rafe exhaled, flabbergasted. "It's a night of surprises. I'm coming." He pushed past Blackthorne and headed above, his first mate behind him, voicing questions. "What other surprises, sir? Have we more trouble coming?"

"Just family business, hidden in the journal. I'll tell you about it later." They both fell silent until they emerged on deck.

Rafe skidded to a stop, staring upward. Blackthorne only just managed to avoid running into him. For there, in the sky about topsail height and trailing the *Jewel* like a pet, floated a Sea Ghoul. Its misty silhouette shimmered in the lantern light and the stars, and it hummed—off-key— the strains of a song vaguely familiar to Rafe. It appeared oddly calm for a creature of its normally angry disposition.

When it caught sight of the captain, the Sea Ghoul slowly drifted towards the deck. Sailors backed away as it passed over the rail and hovered above the wood planks of the ship. Then it bowed its head slightly and spoke.

"God of Souls." Its voice abraded air and ears like a knife scraped against a stone. "Death bade me deliver a message." The timbre of its voice shifted with the next words, sounding almost feminine. "We have run out of time. The Crow comes, in the company of once-dead pirates. Continue south. I will come to you. Meet me at the place they call Cataclysm Reef, in the spot mortals have named Serenity Bay."

With the last word, the Ghoul shot straight into the air and then over the rail, before diving into the depths of the sea. Rafe inhaled and let out his breath with a large sigh.

"Well now. We have our orders I suppose." He turned to Anders, who held the wheel with white knuckles and a mouth open like a dead fish. "You heard the creature, Mr. Anders. We have a rendezvous with Death. Head south to Cataclysm Reef." Anders gawked for a minute, then adjusted the heading, mouth still agape.

Rafe then turned to Blackthorne. "It's a good thing I listened to you and added a spellcaster to the crew. I don't know what scheme the Crow has concocted, but he's coming, with pirates no less, and we should warn the navy." He waved his hand in a sweeping motion. "Shall we?"

With Blackthorne's reply of, "Aye, Captain," the pair went below deck.

They knocked on the door of the spellcaster's quarters,

aft of the ship. Rafe noticed a good luck charm hanging from the doorframe and smiled. One of his sister Lynna's charms. A voice answered with a hearty, yet somehow distracted "Enter", and the two sailors opened the door and walked inside. They found Elwen, their new spellcaster, perched on a stool, arranging bottles in a cabinet.

"Captain Morrow! And Mr. Blackthorne!" Startled exclamations burst from the man, and he fumbled with a bottle, nearly dropping it. He righted the glass container, pushing it onto a cabinet shelf, and quickly climbed off the stool to his feet. "How can I assist you?" He reflexively wiped his hand on a trouser leg and offered it in greeting.

Rafe shook the man's hand, a smile accompanying it. Then Blackthorne followed with another handshake. The three settled down in chairs as Rafe explained why they'd come.

"I need to send two messages. One to King's Rock Fort on Black Shoals and the other to Commander Pelham's new navy patrol fleet. I believe he is currently sailing the waters off Shadow Cay." Rafe tried not to grimace, knowing why Pelham chose that particular island to test his new ships. He paused, trying to compose his next words, but Elwen interjected.

"Do you wish to talk to the navy spellcasters yourself, sir, face to face, or just send a message? I have both crystal stones and a vision mirror."

"Messages will do. Tell them they need to prepare for a possible invasion of pirates, most likely magical or otherworldly in origin. I'm not sure in what numbers, but they should prepare for a sizeable force of an invading enemy. Can you handle that?"

"Um, of course. You, um, did say pirates? Magical pirates? Will they believe, I mean—" He nibbled anxiously on his lip. "My apologies, but will I have to, um, convince them?"

"I shouldn't think so, not after our last skirmish. The navy has become quite the believers in strange happenings."

"Aye, sir. I suppose we all have. I have some paper and ink here and you can write down exactly what you'd like me to relay." He got up and rummaged in another cabinet, bringing back pen and ink, paper and a portable writing desk to the captain. Rafe scribbled down a message and passed the paper to Elwen.

"I'll send these messages immediately."

"Good man." Rafe and Blackthorne rose from their chairs and left Elwen to his work.

Chapter Six
The Gateway

Black Axe Morgan glowered at the Crow and then at the crowd of awakened, resurrected dead milling in the temple's courtyard. "Look at them. Useless lot. All confused and moaning. What am I supposed to do with that bunch? Some of them used to be my crew, gone down with the *Ravager*, done in by Captain Morrow same as me. But now they're hopeless. And the rest of those bloody dregs are as bad. How can I sail with those weak-kneed snivellers? I bet half of them would turn tail first sign of trouble."

"Perhaps." The Crow ruffled his feathers, oddly reminiscent of a shrug. "But the confusion and disorientation will fade. Those former crewmates of yours will be back to their old selves soon. As for the rest..." He stretched out his wings and chuckled. "I'm sure some will be suitable. The others can learn, or become expendable. Now can't they?"

It was Morgan's turn to chuckle. "I like how you think,

birdie. Indeed I do. I can snuff out their restored lives quick enough with this here magic I stole, if they don't fall in line or prove useful. Plenty more I can recruit in Outlaw Keys, if need be, and if you keep your promise to get us off this accursed island." Morgan gave the Crow a veiled look. "Speaking of which, care to enlighten me on your plan?"

"It should be safe enough to show you. They seem to be adjusted well enough to leave on their own for the time being. But we'll need to take a trip. Your arm if you would."

Morgan held out an arm, and the Crow flew up to perch on his limb. Morgan grinned. "Where we headed, then. Back to the tunnels?"

"No. First to the back garden if you please."

Black Axe Morgan tromped around the temple, the Crow clinging to his outstretched arm, until they arrived in a small garden of sadly neglected herbs and half-dead plants that were once vegetables.

The Crow clacked his beak. "Not a gardener, I see."

Morgan shrugged and transferred the bird to a nearby post. "Never had a bent for growing things. Tried keeping his vegetable patch for a while, but I always preferred to steal my food than grow it. Didn't need it in the end. Plenty of fish in these waters and wild forage." He brushed a feather from his jacket sleeve. "Now what?"

"See that stone marker at the far edge of the garden?"

"That odd sundial, you mean?"

"Yes, but not quite a sundial. Though it does illuminate the way." The Crow chuckled. "Go over to it and place your hand on the star-shaped symbol, in the centre of its circle. Then initiate the necromancer's magic."

Morgan scowled. "What are you trying to pull, bird? Setting an ambush? Going to try to fry me with some trick, some trap?"

"Nothing lethal, I assure you. If I wanted you dead, you

would be. I'm more than powerful enough to kill the likes of you these days. However, only the magic of the island's guardian can activate the path to the Gateway. And since you stole that magic, the necromancer's magic, that makes you the only guardian here." The Crow shifted his weight on the post, fluttering his wings slightly. "Unless you wish to remain on this island?"

"All right, all right." Morgan grumbled but walked over to the marker. "But if I die, I ain't leaving this world, but haunting you, bird, for an eternity."

The Crow snickered. "As if your ghost would be able to hurt me."

"Nah, but I'm betting you could see and hear my ghost and I can make myself a right nuisance when I want."

And with those words he slapped his hand down on the etching. His palm glowed green a moment later and a trickle of magic snaked along the stone, down the marker and into the ground. A soft rumble slid along the earth.

"Excellent. Remove your hand now."

Morgan lifted his hand as if scalded, and suddenly the forest beyond the garden parted and a white stone path appeared.

"Perfect. The way to this world's Realm Gateway." The Crow flapped his wings and gave a small caw of delight. "Your arm, please, Mr. Morgan, and we can see to leaving the island and getting you your vengeance."

Morgan backed away from the marker, staring at the path, before trudging back to the Crow and lending his arm for transport. "So what now? We follow the road out there to this place of yourn?"

"Exactly, Mr. Morgan."

"You have some peculiar ways, birdie, I'll say that. Forests that move, appearing paths. Magic takes some getting used to, but can't say it isn't interesting." Morgan moved forward, hesitating only a moment before setting foot to stone and walking down the trail that now wound through the woods.

A good ten minute trek brought them to their destination: a crystalline obelisk. The Crow flew off Morgan's arm and circled the object, cawing triumphantly. "It's here, it's still here! I've won!" The bird swooped down to settle on top of the obelisk, his claws making a clicking sound as he landed.

"And what exactly is the bloody thing that you won? Looks like some old bit of nothing stone to me."

"This, my fine pirate friend, is the key to our vengeance, reclaiming what was stolen from us. This is the way we leave this wretched place and go home!" The Crow leapt into the air and flew a circle around the obelisk, a cackle of laughter trailing his flight.

"Well, now," Morgan replied in a droll tone, unimpressed by the Crow's antics. "How does it work, then?"

The Crow flew down and settled to perch in a nearby tree. "This one's a bit more complicated. Had you killed the necromancer a few years ago, you wouldn't need me. But a meddling god saw fit to remove your former captor's abilities to power the Gateway while keeping his power to unlock it. A very cruel thing." The Crow bobbed his head while fluttering the tips of his wings. "It kept him here, yet dangled escape within his reach. We had that in common, he and I."

"Damn bastard gods are always making life difficult, aren't they?"

"Indeed. Luckily, I found a way around the restriction." The Crow tilted his head. "You'll need to unlock the stone, as you did in the garden, and then I'll take over." He drew in his wings and fluffed his feathers. "Do you see the marking on the side of the obelisk?" At Morgan's nod, he continued. "Find the one that looks like a key made of bone."

Morgan shot the Crow a dark and confused look, but walked over to the obelisk. As he searched, he muttered, "Now how would you know if a squiggly scrawl drawn in the shape of a key was..." He smiled and then chuckled. "Oh. The top of the thing looks like a skull." He glanced over at the Crow. "Found it, now what? Put me hand over it and do the magical shilly-shally?"

"Exactly. Unlock the portal."

Morgan grunted, placing his palm over the engraved key symbol. Green energy flowed through his flesh and into the stone. It sparked against the hard surface, throwing up flashes of light, and an answering glow of silvery grey lit up the obelisk. Wisps of magic danced in the air, threading long tendrils towards the sky, before encircling the column.

"That's enough, Mr. Morgan. Lift your hand. You've succeeded."

Morgan walked back to the Crow without a word, moving his hand behind his back as he came to a stop. The Crow stretched his wings to fly, only to find fingers suddenly around his throat and the sharp blade of a knife at his breast.

"You ain't going nowhere, birdie. And I'm betting you don't want to find out who's faster: me with this knife or you with your magic." Morgan pushed the knife forward and the Crow hissed.

"What are you doing, you fool? You need me to open the Gateway!"

"Aye, I do. But why would you need me once it's open? I let you do your magic and you fly away home, leaving me to rot here. So's I figure we do this together, then maybe I won't gut you."

The Crow fluttered his wings ever so slightly and cawed

softly, almost like a curse. Then he spat, "I can't. I can't go home. Not yet. I still need Captain Morrow or his magic."

"Why? Why do you need him?"

The Crow hissed, but replied, "He's the key to unlock a certain door. You and I can unlock it to go anywhere in this world, but I need his power to open it for another realm."

Morgan loosened his grip, but didn't withdraw the knife. "That's why you made a deal. You want me to draw the bastard out, so's you can take what you need from him. Or trick him somehow. That it? Am I right?"

The Crow hissed again. "Yes."

Morgan guffawed. "Well, you sneaky bird." He abruptly let go of the Crow's neck and pulled away his knife, sliding it back into his belt sheath. "New deal then. Keep your promise. Get us off this island and to some ships we can commandeer, and I'll deliver up Morrow to you. You can suck out all his power and leave him a husk for all I care. I only ask I get the killing blow. I want to slice that bastard's throat and watch him bleed over my deck."

The Crow adjusted his neck back and forth and clacked his beak. "Done. All I want is his power. What you do to him afterwards is no concern of mine."

"Right then. Let's get this Gateway powered and leave this place." Morgan grinned at the Crow, who shook his feathers and flew into the air.

He soared high, winging a circle above the obelisk. Three times around it he flew, then dived and snatched at a wisp of the obelisk's magic, grabbing it in his beak. He swallowed the fragment of energy and landed on top of the monument. He spread his wings, their feather tips now glowing silver. He then turned to Morgan.

"Where in the Outer Islands do you want to go?"

"Not in the Outer Islands. We're headed to Outlaw Keys, east of the Wakefords. Specifically to a place called

Rotter's Bay on Blayburn Isle. It's a secluded beach, not far from a seaport we can raid. If we're lucky, my old cache of weapons will still be there."

"I know the place." Surprised laced the words. "That makes things easier."

The Crow moved his wings, brushing them back and forth, stroking the air and summoning both his shadow magic and the connecting strand of power he swallowed. The obelisk glowed under his feet, pulsing and giving off a subtle warmth. Suddenly, the Crow took flight and shrieked one word: "*Avove!*"

A ring of light shimmered from the ground below and shot upward towards the sky. The Crow took flight, racing to the clouds, to circle back and return to his tree. There, he and Morgan watched the light ring transform into a whirlwind of luminescence and engulf the obelisk, before it altered stone and air into a massive archway of energy. A small sigh of breath left the Crow, and he said, "Show us Rotter's Bay."

Colour shifted through the energy—green and blue, hues of brown and yellow—until a calm scene of a beach reflected in the shimmering surface. The smell of sea and fish travelled on a sudden breeze and the faint sound of the tide could be heard.

"Well, I'll be a scraped barnacle." Morgan grinned. "Don't that beat all. Rotter's Bay, clear as a bell, and as close as me stubble." He moved forward, peering at the suspended image, and then walked around the archway. "It's just like a painting." He brushed a hand in the air behind the arch. "Only hanging there with both sides the same. What do we do now? Just step into it? Like they do to cross to the After World?"

"Basically the same thing, yes." The Crow moved slightly on his branch. "Only this one works both ways.

Now that we've made a connection, we can reopen it from Rotter's Bay, if we have a need."

Morgan grunted. "I like that. Always good to have a retreat plan. Just in case." He walked back over to the Crow. "It's done, then. Let's go get those scallywags of the dead and get the damnation out of here!"

Chapter Seven
Death Arrives

Mist swirled across the sea around the Isle of Shadows. Thick, grey, and tinted in red, it rolled into shore, hiding the sunlight and bringing a sour smell to the fresh, balmy air. From the ethereal in-between, Cylla, gatekeeper of the isle, shivered and an involuntary whimper escaped her lips.

"Death."

Silence echoed after the name, and then a voice reverberated like thunder across the connected worlds.

"I am coming. No need to open the gates. I will find my own way."

Cylla whimpered again, sinking into the shadows of the realms, letting Death pass by, afraid of her dark gaze.

But Death paid her no heed. She travelled on, in gloom, fog and cold, to a deserted beach on the near side of the Isle of Shadows. The island stilled for her, its shifting nature temporarily halted as Death came ashore. There, a lone figure waited for her.

He spoke, as her black-cloaked form materialized on the sand. "Welcome back."

She looked at him, something akin to warmth in her eyes. "Hello, Reis. I missed you."

He smiled. "I missed you, as well. It has been too long."

For a moment they remained motionless, staring at each other, centuries sloughing off their shoulders, both transported back to when they were together. Then the moment broke and the weight of their two worlds returned. They both resumed their respective burdens and their seasoned masks fell back into place.

Reis broke the silence first. "We have reached our destiny, then? What little I foresaw is now upon us?"

"It seems so. As you know, the Nightmare Crow succeeded in stealing my first son's power. He is Shadow Bird again. Now he stalks our son to steal his power and fly back to the stars."

"Still, after all these centuries, he only thinks of my former home. Only of Ulerne and the Realm of the Stars. The poor creature." Reis sighed.

"Do not feel sorry for him. He had other choices."

Reis shook his head. "And you are still angry at him. Still unforgiving."

Death glared, a look that would have terrified anyone, made them cower and screech. Yet, Reis only smiled. Death exhaled a breath of ice. "Sometimes I am angry. Sometimes I have forgiven. Today it is hard. I have the memory of Ashetus and now he threatens Morrannan."

"Yes, the Crow must be stopped. There is so much at stake. I only wish our son could be spared what is to come. Spared his destiny." Another sigh. "You've given him the journal? And the map?"

"I sent it along with our daughter. I will see her later and make sure it was delivered."

"Good. I have made the other arrangements. You are ready?"

"I am. I have sent word. The meeting with our son will happen."

"I'm sorry I will miss that. Your reunion will be most interesting, I think. Though I believe it will not go quite as you would wish. Try not to upset him."

A rumble issued from her mouth, a sound one could almost characterize as laughter. "We will see. I'm sure he will have questions. Ones I've waited a long time to answer."

"We both have. Fair journey, Death. Until we meet again." He nodded, and she smiled. Then she swirled away in a puff of smoke and fog, headed far from the Isle of Shadows into the mortal world.

A cold wind blew across Red Reef, rattling the thatch and shingles of the village houses and farms that scattered across the island. Waves rocked the fishing boats and shivers chased up the spines of every person, living or dead, on the island. All inhabitants, for a reason they could not explain, scurried indoors, hiding from the icy breeze and the grey clouds gathering in the sky.

For on that wind travelled Death.

Through dark pathways and cracks in the realms she walked, in grey and shadow until her footsteps passed the world veils and trod on solid earth and she breathed the air of mortal beings. She stood on a cliff of Red Reef, her black cloak fluttering in the sea breeze, the sun shining on her pale flesh from behind the dreary clouds. A nearby sheep bleated at her before running away. She watched it go, bemused.

"Strange-looking creature." Her voice shuddered the air, all sharp and angles, churning turmoil and quivering the grass. She sniffed, her nose wrinkling in distaste. "No decay. No rot. Fresh. Sweet. No choking fumes." She sighed, a breath of bleak eons and lament. Then she peered at the sky from beneath her hood. "Light. I hate the Light. And so warm."

She snapped her fingers and the clouds darkened, blotting out the sunlight, and the sky became as twilight. Another snap and the air dropped in temperature, changing to a frosty chill.

"Much better." A rictus of a smile creaked across her bony face. "Still too much light, but better."

She closed her eyes and inhaled, then gradually exhaled with a dash of her shadows on her breath. Beneath her feet the ground trembled and a cracking noise echoed. Slowly, slowly, as her breath moved into the air, the edges of two realms touched and Death reached out with her power. And there, beyond the visible and the tangible, an answering giggle mingled with Death's spectral exhalation.

"Hello, daughter." Tension in Death's shoulders relaxed. "I am waiting. At a place you call Red Reef."

"I know. I know. Can feel you. Be there soon." Another giggle. "A minute or two. Through the cracks. There and back."

The rumble and cracking ceased as Death sighed and pulled in her power. She stared out to sea as she waited for her daughter to arrive. "So different here, yet the sea is the same." Musings and mumblings spewed from her lips, chasing away a curious seabird that had flown in for a closer look. "The sea. With its secrets, with its depths. Both sons loved the sea."

Shadows swirled, shifting between the folds of her cloak, and the surrounding space grew darker. Memories sad and dripping regret surfaced, and for a moment the sunlight itself shivered.

Then a laugh broke the spell and a flash of silver-tinged white shone in the sky. The Goddess of the Moon twirled down from a fissure in the clouds to land gracefully on the cliff side beside her mother. She immediately sat down on the grass and stared up at Death.

"Hello, Mother."

Death looked down at her, puzzled. "What are you doing?"

"Sitting." Manume peered around her mother's form. "Did you know there's a sheep hiding in the woods behind you?"

Death frowned. "What's a sheep?"

Manume laughed again and flopped down on her back, looking up at the clouds. "You've made it very dark in the daytime. Like home. Very nice, even if there's no moon."

Death sighed in exasperation and the grass twitched. The Goddess of the Moon didn't seem to notice. Death waited, staring at her daughter, until finally she broke the silence, asking, "Did you fetch what I asked you to bring? And talk to Bevire?"

"Yes and yes. Talked to sister. She and the Grey Sisters agreed to watch the nasty bird here and there. Shouldn't get caught if they're careful." Manume swished a hand against the grass. "And I brought the thing. Strange thing. Got it and brought it. Or rather Hugh got it. The winged hissing things and those two-headed dogs like Hugh better than me. So I sent him. He fetched it for us. He's nice, Hugh is, and useful, if too sensible. I like him."

A small grumble sounded in Death's throat, not quite a growl. "What is a Hugh?"

"Not a what, silly mother, a who. Hugh the who. He is my friend. A ghost. A friend and a ghost. He used to be my brother's, now he's mine."

"You have a ghost? Odd." Death's cloak swished.

"Yes, he is odd but helpful." Manume reached into a pocket of her skirts and plucked out a conch shell.

"Good. Hand it to me if you would."

Manume scrambled to her feet and presented the shell to her mother with a flourish. "Why do you need an old shell?"

"This is very special." She traced a finger over the alabaster surface. "It's a piece of the old realm." Death held the object in her palm and breathed on it. Shadows danced off her tongue and entwined around the exterior, fusing a tiny bit of darkness into the shell.

She held it out to the Moon Goddess. "Your turn. Add a drop of moonlight, if you will." Manume touched a finger to the conch and her light wrapped around the outside. "Excellent. Now I need you to take this to the Grey Sisters and Bevire. I need them to build me something from its essence." Death smiled, leaning in to whisper in her daughter's ear.

Manume smiled in return. "Oh, clever mother. Naughty mother. I like this thought." She took back the conch shell and stepped away. "Off to the Grey Sisters, then." In a flash of pale silver and a wisp of a sigh from Death, the Goddess of the Moon vanished.

And far to the south, the *Celestial Jewel* sailed towards Cataclysm Reef and Serenity Bay. Death lingered for a moment on the cliff, reaching out quietly to sense her son. Above his ship, clouds suddenly darkened and the air grew icy. Everyone on board shivered and Rafe looked at the sky.

Death smiled, knowing her son was there. She stepped off the cliff and left Red Reef to make her rendezvous, with a small detour before she met her remaining son. She sailed across the sky, over the sea, trailing shadows and subconscious fear in her wake.

51

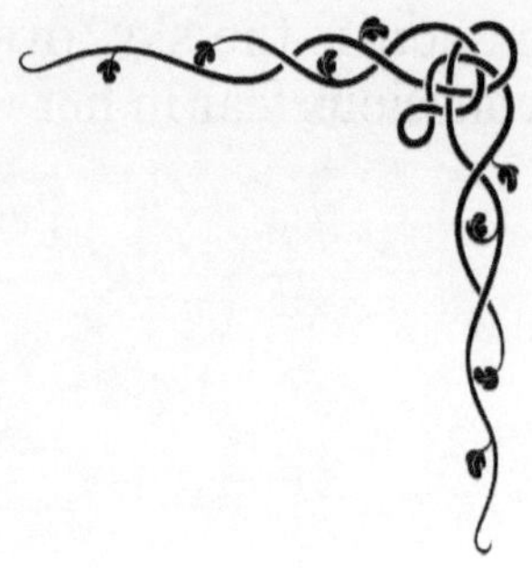

Chapter Eight
The Pirates Are Coming

Anchored in Serenity Bay, the *Celestial Jewel* bobbed in the waters of the harbour, alight in the morning sun. A still calm blanketed the ship as they awaited the coming of Death. Apprehension chased the crew, mingling with repose, the trepidation of their expected guest warring with the beauty and languor of the day. Most of the men gathered on deck to bask in the sunlight and air, yet the captain was conspicuously absent topside.

Rafe was below decks, in his quarters, feet on his desk, a glass of wine near at hand, reading his father's words from a journal.

It was most strange, moving an island. Taking a tiny piece of the Archipelago and shifting it across the sea. Not at all like when we all created that sanctuary. That was simply hiding one realm from another, putting up barriers. This felt more like slicing off a piece of something, like stealing it. Though the denizens of the Archipelago seemed glad to see it go. I think the place reminded them too much of Ulerne's arrival and his continued visits. They are glad to be left to themselves, to have peace.

"Why would he need to move an island from the Archipelago?" Rafe mused aloud and took a gulp of wine. He turned the page and kept reading.

I found a safe place, south of the mortals and their homes, for the island and the Gateway. The man who agreed to be its guardian journeys there. He will use the spell I granted him and set up the shroud to hide it from prying eyes. He has also agreed to bind his magic to seal the gate from strangers and those who would misuse it. Once that is done, my father will never be able to use it again. No one will, save myself, the guardian, and his successors. And even in that, I decided to limit the ability to utilize the gate. It will work in this realm, but not to travel beyond our new world. It is too dangerous now.

Rafe stopped reading, mumbling, "This Gateway again?" Rafe shivered, a familiarity scratching against his memory. "Is it a portal between realms? Why have I never heard of this? Yet, it feels like I know…" He frowned, teeth grinding in frustration. "And shrouding it? Wait. The other journal… What if…" Words dribbled away as realization dawned in his brain. He snapped the book shut and yanked open a desk drawer, pulling out the map his sister had given him. His feet dropped from the desk and he rolled out the chart, studying the odd symbols and runes. Then he tapped a finger on the wide marking at the top.

"I bet that represents the Great Southern Mists." A stinging tingle traced against his skin and he jerked his hand away, frowning. He moved his fingers back along the paper but nothing happened. He turned his attention back to the symbols.

One in particular caught his eye. Faint, old, in a script he had nearly forgotten. The symbol of a gateway. With a laugh, he stabbed his finger on the spot on the map.

"There! That is your hidden island, Father, with your Gateway. Isn't it?" Rafe leaned back in his chair, shaking his head. "Why go to all that trouble to protect it? Was Grandfather that bad?"

Rafe rolled up the map, and placed it back in the drawer, shutting it away. He drained his glass of wine and poured himself another. He stared at the journal, but didn't pick it up, his mind trying to fathom what other secrets it held. Instead, he left it on his desk, grabbed the wine bottle and went up on deck.

❖

"All right, you lot, let me explain how things is going to be!"

Black Axe Morgan barked at a ragged assembly of the formerly dead lined up in rows on the beach of Rotter's Bay. The necromancer's former experiments swayed and shifted their feet, while rusty weapons from Morgan's stash clinked around their waists. The Crow, perched on a low-hanging branch, watched the spectacle from the shade of a copse of trees.

"Each one of you scum was plucked from the sea and death by that bastard necromancer and brought back into damned life by his dark magic. Well, I got that magic now!" Morgan stretched out a hand, sparked a flame of green energy and then extinguished it. "So you lot are mine now! You answer to me, you scallywags! Anyone got a problem with that?"

Silence reigned over the beach.

"Good! Shows your sense got resurrected with you."

His tone suddenly softened. "Now I know it's a rum thing, what happened." He slowly began to pace the rows, looking his men in the eyes. "Some got better deals than others. Some of you came back with holes in your flesh, missing parts and..." He paused, sniffed and continued, "well...bits of rot. Don't matter none to me. You can still sail in *my* crew. We're the same. We're the dead that was, but ain't no more." A shuffling of feet and even a faint cheer sounded. Then a cough and a question.

A young man with a missing eye and half a head of straw-coloured hair spoke up. "Sir, what are we going to do exactly, sailing with you?"

Morgan strode over to the youth and glared. "We be doing pirating! You got a problem with that?"

The youth shook his head. "No, sir! Got no problem with that! Name's Finn. Ain't nothing I like better than stealing!" Finn grinned, adding, "'Cept maybe killing folks first."

Morgan laughed and slapped Finn on the shoulder. "A lad after my own black heart. Glad to have you as part of my crew. I love the vicious ones." He then stepped back and shouted, "Anyone here object to a bit of pirating!"

Whether out of fear or compliance, not a no, nay or any other negative came as a reply. Morgan grinned. "Well then, let's go pay the town of Briar Glen a visit." He yanked his sword from its sheath and waved it in the air. "We'll pillage the place! And steal us some ships!"

A croaking cheer rose off the beach and a shambling, straggling crew of half-men followed Morgan as he strode across the sand, headed to the path that led to the sea port of Briar Glen.

The Crow watched them go before flying after them with a laugh.

A young boy saw them first, a lad going to Rotter's Bay to fish for crabs. He met the would-be pirate horde on the path, and Black Axe Morgan sliced his throat with his sword before the youth could cry a warning. Morgan shoved the hapless boy's corpse into the weeds for the carrion eaters and signalled his men to keep moving.

The company trampled grass and dirt in relative silence, trudging along the path, rising over a hillock until they viewed Briar Glen. A quiet, peaceful town full of ordinary people going about their day. Most fishermen were out at sea, though a few stayed in port mending nets or boats. Buyers and sellers haggled in the open marketplace and faint strains of music chimed across the wind from the music pavilion. And in the harbour, Black Axe Morgan spied three docked ships ripe for the taking.

He pointed to their prize. "See those beauties, boys? That's our final destination. Two-masted rigging, sleek hulls, probably smaller cargo ships. No doubt outfitted with light cannon for defence. They'll suit our purposes just fine." He grinned. "We'll raid the town first and take what we want, and then board the ships and seize them."

Finn sidled up to Morgan. "I'm all for that, sir, but do ye have a plan? I doubt the townsfolk will put up much of a fight, but the sailors won't go down easy. I mean, ain't none of us want to end up dead again, I reckon."

"It'll take a bit more to kill ya now, lad, than a sword or a club. But you're right about town. We'll cut through them like butter. As to the ships..." Morgan grinned at Finn, raising his hand. It lit up in green fire, and pointed upward at the Crow, who circled the sky above the men. "You leave the sailors to me and the birdie. We'll do the main killing and you lot can mop up the stragglers."

He laughed and drew his sword, the blood of the boy he killed smeared on the blade. He thrust it into the air with a cry of, "Attack! Send them all to the After World," and charged, screaming down upon the town. His horde of resurrected dead charged after him, their murderous cries echoing past the sea and shattering the peaceful afternoon.

They barrelled into the east side of the town, rushing from a copse of trees, screeching like madmen and brandishing weapons, all to terrorize the townsfolk. People panicked, and pirates cut them down in the streets as they stormed through, sometimes stripping jewelry and valuables from the bodies as they went. The attack caused chaos—the stench of blood filled the air, mixing with the sound of shrieks and the thump of trampling feet as victims tried to escape—but met little resistance until they broke through into the town square. There, a small company of armed guards waited, swords at the ready. Nine men with pale faces, blades trembling in their hands and fear in their eyes.

Morgan called a halt to the advance of his own men and smiled. "Well, well, what have we here? A citizen's guard? Not navy men and not trained by the look of those shaking hands. Looks to me like fresh meat, boys. Have at 'em!"

Morgan roared with laughter as his company surged forward and cut the nine guards to ribbons and looted their corpses. Blood, brains and limbs scattered across the cobblestones and Morgan walked through the gore with a grin.

"Let's check out the marketplace next, boys, and see if the fine folk of Briar Glen left us anything to pillage!" Then he looked up. "Crow! Go make sure those ships ain't left! Keep 'em there if you can!" Circling overhead, the Crow laughed and swooped away, flying towards the docks. Morgan signalled his men, crying, "To the marketplace!"

They arrived to empty streets and stalls, the word of

their invasion having caused the vendors and buyers to flee in fear of their lives; many left behind wares and money. Morgan's pirates ransacked the stalls, destroying some for fun, ripping them apart as they stole coin and anything of value they could stuff in their pockets and satchels. Finn held up a fist full of pendants from a jeweller's stall, a grin plastered on his blood-streaked face.

"Some fancies, Captain! And coin aplenty!"

Morgan smiled at being called captain again. It had been too long. "And more to come, young Finn, once we take our ships! We'll stock the holds with stores, coins and fancies and loot everything we want from this town! And then we'll raid the next town, and the next and the next!"

A cheer rose on the wind, and Morgan led his band of bloodthirsty pirates to the port.

The docks were deserted when they arrived, the harbourmaster and the dock crews having fled, but the three ships still floated gently in their berths, awaiting the pirates' arrival. A strange black mist surrounded them, and the Crow sat perched on a wharf post. Aboard the vessels, frightened sailors stood on deck, armed with swords and knives and manning the harpoons.

"The ships didn't leave, Mr. Morgan, as requested." The Crow chuckled.

Morgan laughed in return. "A fair trick, that, Crow. A grand trick. Now let me show you some of mine. A bit of spell magic from our old friend, the necromancer."

Morgan closed his eyes, his fingers flashing green fire. He whispered, "*Inrydd.*"

An unhallowed glow crept up the sides of the ships, like the slow seep of the tide under a dock. It slid over the wood onto the decks, slithered along the mast and rigging, seeking the crew in its gradual yet relentless invasion. Sailors ran from it screaming, trying to hide, to no avail;

the glow slid against flesh and bone trapping the men in its grip. Morgan waited until the magic finished its work and whispered again.

"*Igolsi.*"

The three ships erupted in a burst of energy and horrific screams that shattered the air of the Briar Glen port. As the pirates watched with glee, every sailor on the ships turned to grey ash, their bodies consumed in an instant, transformed from flesh to cinders. Their powdered remains swirled upward: from the decks, from the bowels of the vessels, out from every crack and crevice, and blew out to sea on a green-tinged wind.

"Well, birdie? What do ya think? Like me trick?" Morgan tapped his foot impatiently and sported a satisfied grin.

The Crow stretched his wings and clacked his beak. "Most impressive, Mr. Morgan. The Smoldering Flesh. Not many can master that spell." The Crow leapt in the air and flew to the top of a mast. "Come take your spoils, Mr. Morgan, or should I say, Captain."

Morgan's grin grew wider. "You heard the birdie, crew! To the ships!"

◆

Back on the dock, after securing his newly captured vessels, Morgan watched his men drag a prisoner towards him. They dumped the clearly beaten man at his feet. Morgan gave the man a kick.

"Look at me!"

The shaking man raised his head, scrambling to his knees. Morgan spat on him.

"So you're the Lord Mayor of Briar Glen. My men tell me you tried to flee. Sent more guard out to fight while you tried to escape with the gold and other coin!"

The cowering man nodded.

Black Axe Morgan backhanded his face, the smack of his hand rattling the Lord Mayor's teeth and snapping his head back. "You thought you could run! With money I wanted! My money! Nobody takes what's mine!"

The man whimpered and whined. "Please, please, I'm sorry! I didn't mean it! I panicked! You can have it. We won't fight anymore! No more guard! Take what you want! We won't resist. No need to kill anyone else. What you did to those poor men…" The mayor retched. "Take anything! Take it all! Just spare us!" The broken man grovelled on the docks, head lowered, staring at Morgan's feet. The pirate captain kicked him in the side and the man rolled over on to his back and moaned.

"I don't need the say-so of a weak-kneed coward like you to pillage this town. I'm Black Axe Morgan! My name sent fear through the blood of everyone alive in the Outer Islands!" He kicked the mayor again and the man cried out in pain. "Some mayor you are, running from your grand office, trying to flee, 'til my men dragged you back and through the streets." Morgan spit again, the wet glob landing in the mayor's hair. "A leader would have come on his feet! Only cowards get hauled about like a sack of meal." Morgan landed another kick. The man shrieked this time. "And what's more, I'll kill whoever I please. Starting with you!"

Morgan stomped his boot on the man's head over and over, a thumping rhythm echoing with the mayor's screams. The pirate smashed bone and blood into the dock and smeared the wood with the brains of the former Lord Mayor of Briar Glen.

Then he stepped over the body and strode across the dock, trailing blood and yelling, "No one tells Black Axe Morgan what to do and who to kill! And no one tries to take what I want! I do the taking! It's time this world learned to fear my name again!"

Then he stopped and whirled to face the ships and his gathered pirates. His face held an expression that could curdle the blood of the dead. "Finn!" The lad stepped forward. "What stores and provisions do we have for the ships?"

Finn snapped to attention. "We raided all the dockside alehouses and the town's cold stores, plus the more well-to-do residences. We got plenty of stores to last us weeks, sir. Plus, we filled the coffers from the taverns and the Lord Mayor's home."

"Good. That's a start." Morgan's mouth turned up into a half-smile, half-snarl. "But we're taking it all. Assemble men! As many as you need. Go from home to home. Spread the word. Every citizen of Briar Glen is to bring me their coin, their jewels, their wool and other goods. I want every last thing of value this dinky town has to offer! If they protest, kill 'em! If they resist, kill 'em! I want this town raided bare and all of it loaded into our ships!"

As a giddy Finn jumped to obey the order, Morgan added one more thing to his command. "And hogtie a few of the most prominent citizens and haul them back here to the docks. I want to give this town a little show."

Pirates brandishing swords surrounded a crowd of Briar Glen's people as they were lined up to view Morgan's show. Some shivered, others stared at the ground, and some wore garments still stained with blood. Earlier, they had watched their money and possessions disappear into the holds of stolen ships, handed over to the thieves at sword point. Now they waited, prisoners, forced to bear witness to Morgan's macabre spectacle.

Muffled noises came from the edge of the harbour docks. Three members of the Briar Glen council, two men and a woman, were strung up on the signal posts, bound and gagged. Morgan stood beside his captives, sword drawn. He tapped his foot and addressed the other townsfolk.

"People of Briar Glen. Your town is mine. But some of yer fellows think otherwise. They show disrespect. They don't fear me." Morgan scowled. "This displeases me. For I am a man to be feared. So, you're here on this dock to witness my displeasure and learn a lesson. Why Black Axe Morgan is the terror of the seas."

He lifted his sword and stuck it in the abdomen of one of the men tied to the posts. The man screamed and continued to scream as Morgan slit him open until his guts bulged out. The wounded man choked on blood for a few minutes before passing out. His body twitched as blood and bile discharged from his stomach. Beside him, the other two bound prisoners shrieked and shook against their ropes. Their shrieks got louder as Morgan slit them open as well before their cries turned into choking moans. Morgan laughed and once again addressed the now screeching and retching crowd, yelling to be heard above the din.

"See these folks?" He pointed at the three mutilated people. "They'll die slow and painful. Blood seeping out, guts spilling out. Why? Because *I* wanted it. Because *I* enjoyed doing it. Remember that! Remember Black Axe Morgan likes killing! Do what I tell ya, when I tell ya, or I'll chop ya all into pieces!" His frenzied laugh echoed across the dock, and then he shouted, "Let 'em go boys! Send 'em scurrying back to the rest with their tales of horror!"

His men lowered their swords, grins on their faces, and let the townspeople run, the dock emptying faster than wind blowing beach sand. Morgan watched them go, satisfied he made his point. Behind him came the soft groans of the dying.

Morgan pulled a cloth out of his pocket and wiped the blood and residue off his blade before sheathing the weapon. He tossed the stained fabric away and strode forward, shouting.

"Did ye see them run, the spineless rabble? They'll spread the word! And make sure the next lot gets a good gander at them bodies up on the posts! Make sure they know what fate awaits them if they cross me!" He spied Finn and walked over, clapping the youth on the back. "Ah, boy, it feels good to be back in the world instead of stuck on the island toadying to that bastard necromancer. Can't wait to sail the seas again and wreak more havoc. First the Outlaw Keys, then the Wakefords and then headed home to the Outer Islands, killing and stealing as we go!"

"Aren't you forgetting something?" Behind him, a voice echoed, and Morgan looked around to see the Crow perched on a stack of crates. "As amusing as your bloodthirsty antics are, I opened the gate so you could seek out and fight Captain Morrow, not go on a pirate spree. I thought you wanted revenge?"

"Oh, birdie. I haven't forgotten. Why do ye think I put on a show? Let the bodies pile up? The more carnage we leave in our wake, the greater the chances he hears about how Black Axe Morgan's returned from the dead. Why seek him out when we can make him come to us? On our terms. Into our trap." Morgan chuckled. "And have some fun while we're doing it."

"Ah." The Crow ruffled his feathers with the reply. "Sound reasoning. I do prefer it when the enemy walks into his own demise." Then he flew off, his words trailing, "I do hope, for your sake, it happens that way."

Morgan glared, but said nothing. He only watched the Crow settle onto a ship's mast with fury in his eyes.

As the ships left port the next morning, Morgan stood at the quarterdeck rail on his rechristened ship, the *Shadow Raider*. He stared at the bodies still tied to the wharf posts and laughed as the passing vessels scattered the buzzing flies and carrion birds that feasted on their bloodied remains. He turned back to his crew as they sailed past the edge of the bay, his gleeful voice shouting, "Onward to raid, boys! Time to let the world know about Black Axe Morgan and his pirates!"

Chapter Nine
Meetings and Mothers

After midday passed and there was still no sign of his mother, Rafe went back to his quarters and picked up the journal. He stared at it for a good ten minutes, the leather and pages gripped tightly in his fingers before finally opening it to read.

It is done. The guardian has hidden the island with a barrier of mist, much the same trick I used with the Archipelago, though a lesser version of the spell. No one will be trapped, only turned back, unable to get through. This time there was no need to feed the darkness to keep it enclosed.

Rafe sucked in a breath, his eyes devouring the words, his thoughts swirling.

The Gateway is sealed as well, although with far more consequence. Ulerne knew. The moment the guardian snapped the spell in place and barricaded it with our magic, my father tried to break what we had done. He failed, but I heard his scream of rage reverberate through the veil of the realms. My former home is lost to me. I will never see the Realm of the Stars again. My father will never forgive this betrayal. But he is not the only one angry. The Shadow Bird...

Rafe flipped the page as a rapid knock sounded on his door. Irritated, he glanced up and barked, "What is it?"

Blackthorne's anxious voice rang out, "I think your mother's here, sir. The weather... Well, come see for yourself."

Rafe dropped the book and jumped to his feet. He raced across his quarters, yanked open the door and dashed past Blackthorne without a word.

As he burst on deck, his skin shivered, a frosty wind swirling past and around the ship. Sunlight faded into charcoal-grey clouds and the seas lay still and flat as glass. Not a leaf blew from the island trees, despite the wind, nor a blade of grass or grain of beach sand. The air felt stale and heavy with the faint scent of rot. Any shadows that crept from the corners seemed darker than the Stone Fire Islands swamp tar.

Rafe held his breath and waited. Sure enough, a black swarm of mist snaked across the sea, a seething mass of writhing miasma and gloom surrounding a tall, thin silhouette. As the apparition passed the *Jewel*, headed for the shore, every man—save Rafe—trembled, some even whimpered or shut their eyes. Fear wafted in her wake.

Death had come to see her son.

The shadows swept over the beach and dissipated, leaving a lone cloaked figure. She turned to look at the ship, waiting. Rafe took a breath to steady his nerves and summoned his magic. He hovered gently over the deck for a minute, before rising over the rail and floating inland to the shore. He landed facing his Mother and gave her a pained smile. A flood of words tumbled from his mouth.

"I'm here. Care to explain all this? Why have you come to this world from your dark realm? What is going on and what trouble is coming?"

"Not even a hello for your mother?" A cold wind blew between them. "Even your mad sister had a hello for me."

Rafe scowled and then sighed. "Fine. Hello, Mother." He kicked at the sand. "Now what are you up to and what's going on?"

"I've told you already. The Nightmare Crow is coming for you." She tilted her head. "The creature has set events into motion to draw you out and lure you into his trap. You mustn't be fooled. Not by weakness or sentiment. I've come to aid you, to prepare you for what you must do." She smiled, a dark, sickly grimace. "Do what I tell you and all will be well."

Repressing a shiver, Rafe straightened his spine. "Does this aid include telling me the truth?" Rafe didn't keep the bitter sting out of his words. "The things I've learned. All the lies you and Father have been telling about our family history. Why should I believe anything you say?"

The shadows around Death twitched, but she simply replied, "Have you been reading the diary?"

Rafe nodded. "But that's not the only place I've found the truth."

Death shook her head, cold wind swirling. "So dark little secrets are surfacing, are they?" She laughed softly and the trees shivered. "Read the rest of the journal if you want your truth. It matters not to me." She stared at her son. "What does matter is you received the map as well."

"I did." Rafe snorted, annoyed at his mother's

dismissal and change of subject. "For all the good of it. None of the markings make sense, except a rune showing the location of the Gateway. We haven't deciphered any more of it and it certainly won't help us navigate through the Great Southern Mists." Rafe scowled. "Another one of your dark secrets, I suppose. Perhaps it's time to give them up and provide me with some answers." He clenched his jaw, adding, "No more lies."

Death twitched again and the tide formed a slight sheen of ice along the beach. "Is the map on board your ship?"

Rafe curled his lip. "Yes, but that map is just another pointless bit of puzzle and subterfuge. Stop avoiding the issue!"

Death sighed and Rafe felt his heart slow for a minute fraction of a second. She replied, "There is no issue. We did what we did. No more than that."

She stared at him, her eyes timeless voids of shrieking bleak night, her face stern and grim. For a moment Rafe felt as if he were a rodent in the paw of a cat. Uncomfortable memories bounced in his brain and centuries of age fell away, leaving him a naughty child hiding from his mother. He looked away, staring at his feet.

Death placed a cold finger under his chin and lifted his head. She smiled. "Every parent lies to their children. There are things children cannot know until they are grown. The lies of gods are just bigger."

Rafe pulled away from her touch, angry at her and himself. "I've been grown for some time. Yet you still lied."

"Are you now?" Death sounded amused. "All grown up? Yet you still play make-believe. Sailing about with mortals. Years you may have, but ever have you refused to be a god. And you ask that we would trust you with godly things? Why would we do such a thing?"

Rafe scowled. "I never refused to be a god, Mother. Only your type of god. Sealing myself away from the world. Hiding and sulking in a dark corner. Like a child." Rafe smirked as he said the last words, jabbing at his mother's haughty demeanour.

She gasped and narrowed her eyes. The skies above turned black with murky, frenzied clouds. "I never hid from anything or anyone!" The wind whipped a gale across the beach, sending up sprays of sand and rattling the trees. "I retreated from a world where I no longer belonged."

Rafe gazed at her, distress in his eyes, swallowing and biting at his lip. "A mother always belongs with her children."

Death turned her head and looked towards the sea. "Does she? Even one such as me?" She looked back at her son. "This isn't my world. This isn't even a world that was supposed to be."

Rafe frowned. "What do you mean?"

Death hesitated, and then said, "Dreams and love are a two-edged sword in the hands of creatures of Chaos. We shouldn't be allowed to dream or to care for other beings. These emotions only destroy what we want. Chaos has cursed us, I think, in a jealous spite. Cursed all her offspring and followers."

Rafe gaped, his mouth poised on the edge of words but his mind incapable of swirling his thoughts into a sentence. His mother had never been so...forthright. Silence fell between them.

Death ignored his discomfiture. "That is how it all started. With love and dreams. But it doesn't have to remain that way. Broken and not what it should have been. You can fix it, my son. Turn time back into what it was." Shadows lengthened on the beach and the air seemed to howl. "You need to assume your rightful place as a god. To erase this mistake of a world and bring back the balance of Darkness."

"What are you talking about?" Rafe snapped out of his daze, a familiar unease prickling against his skin.

"I speak of returning this world to its glory. Bringing back the Realm of Eternal Night."

"No!" Rafe snarled and even bared his teeth. His shoulders hunched and he squeezed his fingers into fists. "Not this again. I heard enough of this nonsense as a child. You constantly complained about this world and what you lost. How you wanted the Realm of Eternal Night back. And now you want *my* help with some plan of yours?" Rafe shook his head and stepped back from her. "I say no. This world is not a mistake, and your place of Darkness is *never* coming back!"

Death hissed and clouds blocked out the sun, turned day into twilight. "You have no choice! It is time for you to achieve your destiny!"

"My destiny?" Rafe recoiled, his arm moving as if to push her away or ward off evil. "Who are you to tell me my destiny? If your vision of the worlds is my future, then I want no part of it."

Death bristled. "Always with the same refrain. Even as a child. You refuse to accept your responsibilities. You were born for greatness, yet you threw away your power and refused to take my place as keeper of this realm." Death paused, black mist rising off the sand. "You can no longer run away. You must undo what has been done. To restore what is mine!"

Rafe flinched, then pinched his lips together and scowled. "What was yours is long gone, Mother."

"No it isn't!" Death screeched. The ground quaked in response and the seas tossed as if in the beginning throes of a storm. "You are this realm's salvation!"

Rafe clenched his jaw. "As long as I do what you say."

"Yes." Death swished the edge of her cloak, her eyes shining, a glossy black.

"That will never happen." Rafe straightened his spine, his shoulders moving back and his chin lifting. "I will protect this world and its people, not destroy it."

"Bah." Death snorted. "Always the stubborn one. You were supposed to rule these mortals. Shape them into what we gods wanted, needed. It was your role to dominate this realm, take it back from the Light. For me, for Chaos. Instead you befriended them, lived with them. Let them keep my realm. These lesser things, the least of my creations." Death sneered and the air shuddered. "These mortals came from leftover shadows and dregs of realm magic. They weren't even supposed to exist."

"Weren't they?" Rafe matched her sneer with one of his own. "Yet they do. You look down on them, but you don't even know them."

"Why would I?" Death cast him a puzzled stare, her head tilting to one side. "They are fleeting. Not worth the time of beings such as us." At Rafe's look of disgust, her tone softened. "Don't be angry. They are inconsequential in the grand scheme of things. In the plans I have for your destiny."

"Oh yes, your great plans!" Rafe grimaced. "Mapping out every inch of my life. Only you never bothered to ask what I wanted, if I agreed. Well, I didn't. I never wanted to rule anyone! I befriended the mortals because I wanted to, not because they're lesser beings. I walk among them with compassion when I can and I give them respect when it is deserved. Just because I can destroy everyone, doesn't mean I should. Fear is your way, Mother, not mine! I live among them, defer to their ways, as my choice. The only one I could make and live with myself."

"How very noble. How very naïve. Your presence here only makes their pitiful lives harder. The actions of gods have sweeping consequences. One small act can haunt you years later." Death smiled, cold and heartless.

Rafe frowned. He knew his mother well enough to see she was hiding something. "What actions? What aren't you telling me?"

"Do you really wish to know? How one of your choices played out? You protected mortals, but failed to see the end of the thread. Now your past returns, bringing sweet, sweet slaughter with him."

Rafe felt a chill along his spine. "What happened?"

"A soul you put astray was caught in a net. One of those mortals you prize meddled in godly affairs. Stirred up all sorts of nastiness." Death chuckled. "So you see, mortals are not worthy of you, not worthy of us. They are less than children and need to be herded, penned. They need to be guided." She reached out and touched Rafe's arm. "Stop chasing their foolish lives and follow me. Together we will reshape this world the way it was meant to be."

Rafe steadied his nerves and his anger, resisting the urge to brush off her hand. He repeated, "What happened?"

Death sighed, just a tiny breath, but Rafe felt the cold on his face. "I told you, when I sent my message to bring you here. The pirates. The Crow allied himself with some creature called Black Axe Morgan and—"

"Black Axe Morgan!" Rafe pulled away, shouting, disbelief dripping off his words. "How?"

Death shrugged. "A necromancer."

Rafe turned, looking out towards the sea, towards the *Jewel*. "Where is he now?"

"He, the Crow, and the rest of his band of pirates are in the place you call the Outlaw Keys. The island of Blayburn."

"Then I have to go. That beast of a man cannot be

allowed to roam free again." Rafe moved to leave.

Death snarled and grabbed her son's arm. "No! You must not confront the Crow! I told you it was a trap! This Morgan, he is the bait to lure you in for the kill. I will not let that happen!"

Rafe glared. "You have no say in the matter of what I do." He pulled his arm from her clutch. "I can't leave Morgan out there unchecked."

"That pirate is nothing! There are more important matters! You are needed elsewhere!" Death shrieked and the whole island shook with the reverberation of her desperation. "You must come with me!"

"I must do nothing." Rafe nearly stamped his foot like he had as a child. "I'm leaving to stop Black Axe Morgan, and that is final! Are you prepared to stop me?"

Death hissed. "Do not do this. There will be consequences. You are not ready to face the Crow and his allies. Do not chase this Morgan."

Rafe inhaled a long breath. "What would you have me do? Abandon the innocent to the effects of my mistake instead? You said it yourself. The actions of gods have sweeping consequences."

"Yes. And do not throw my words back at me," Death snapped. "More is at stake than a few paltry mortals."

"Not to me. I'm going." Rafe turned and strode away from her, half expecting her to attack, before rising on his magic and heading towards the Jewel.

Death watched him go, whispering, "There is more at stake, my son, and I cannot let you be distracted. You will do as you are told whether you wish it or not. I have made certain of that."

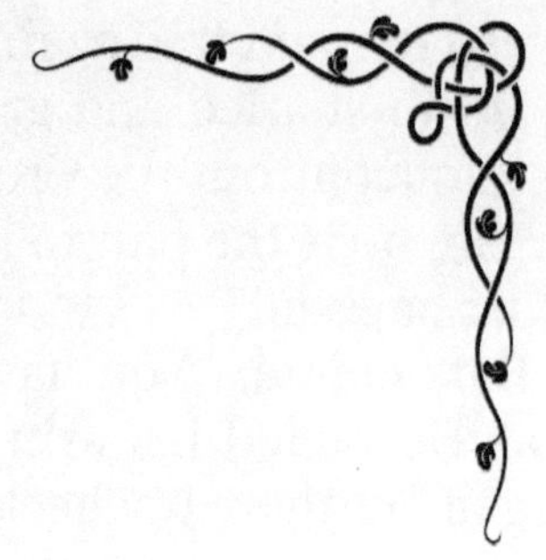

Chapter Ten
Turmoil

After his encounter with his mother, with the *Jewel* sailing at full speed towards Morgan and his pirates, Rafe brooded in his cabin, drinking wine and staring at the journal and tapping his fingers on the leather. After a good half hour of stalling—plus half a bottle of wine consumed—Rafe finally opened the book where he left off.

The Shadow Bird confronted me about moving the island. The creature had been visiting the Gateway in the Archipelago, trying in a vain attempt to return to the Realm of the Stars. I could have told him the efforts would have been useless. He does not possess his full power any longer, and even when he did, it took the combined power of all three Shadow Birds to open it.

And that was before. Now, with the new seal, it is impossible. He did not take that news well. He attacked and threatened me, but I sent him reeling. He flew off in a huff, but I fear he will be back.

I was right. The Shadow Bird returned. But not in anger or aggression. The creature took a different tack. He offered me a gift. A star stone. He said it was one of the remnants that fell to this world with Ulerne's first visit, but I knew better. I could feel it. It was a piece of star magic from Ankara. And no bit of that star ever fell to this realm to become a stone. The cheeky creature must have stolen it somehow. And dared to offer it to me as a bribe.

Rafe paused and drank some wine, digesting both liquor and the disclosure of the Ankara Stone's origin. Then he resumed.

I admired his gall, but he angered me with the insult. I most likely would have thrown his scrawny feathered impertinence across the sea had Death not arrived. She was fury itself, and we both cowered from her. I had never seen her so enraged, so hurt. I thought for a moment she meant to kill the Shadow Bird, but she only banished the creature. Sealed the Isle of Shadows from his sight and locked him in the world of mortals. I barely had time to grab the Ankara star stone from his claws before she unleashed her ferocity. It was not a good day for the Shadow Bird.

Rafe's fingers tightened their grip on the book, the pressure indenting the edges of the pages. His mind swirled at all the family secrets bubbling to the surface. As much as he hated it, one thought kept bouncing around in his mind.

Have my parents lied to me my whole life?

He clenched his jaw and flipped the journal onto his desk, upside down and still open. He filled his wine glass and drank it down, barely taking a breath. Some strange, elusive awareness still itched at the back of his mind. He glared at the leather-bound receptacle of truth and disillusion.

"Was anything they told me as a child true? My great heroic grandfather? A lie. Hiding the existence of the Gateway? Another way of lying. And the Shadow Bird?" Rafe ground his teeth and hissed. "You banished him entirely, until he came back as the Nightmare Crow to make trouble. And you still held back the facts. Only now do you tell the truth because it forced itself out of the shadows." Rafe laughed harshly at his own weak joke. "You and Mother are cut from the same cloth. Ever moving pieces on the game board to suit your own ends." Rafe pushed the diary away, the book sliding a few inches across the desk. "You talk of the Shadow Bird, but you are no better than him, with your schemes and plans, and manipulations of my life."

He eyed the wine bottle, but placed his empty glass on the desk. Rafe shoved his chair back, rose and stalked out of his quarters to the decks above. He stormed up the steps to the quarterdeck, weaving slightly, and leaned on the rail, staring into the heaving waves surrounding the ship.

"Blackthorne!" He shouted his first mate's name in a tone as black as his disposition. "How long until we reach the Outlaw Keys? I'm in the mood to vanquish some pirates."

"Even at top speed, most likely two days, sir,"

Blackthorne's even voice did nothing to calm Rafe's ire, nor did the beauteous day or rolling water and salt spray. For a moment he thought to rise above it all and make his own way there, to leave ship and crew behind and let the full fury of his godly prowess reign down on his enemies. His fingers tightened on the rail, a slight blue glow shining against the wood.

Then it faded and he lifted his head, looking out across the sea, Cataclysm Reef in the distance.

That's what you want, isn't it? For me to abandon everyone and become this vengeful, fearsome god. Or some omnipotent deity, aloof and full of secrets. To become just like you. Death and the Sovereign of Gods, always with your lies and your plans. Well, I won't be like you. Not ever.

Rafe took a breath and turned around with what he hoped was a cheery smile. "Very good. I'll be in my quarters if anyone needs me."

He brushed past Blackthorne and the other crew, rushed down the steps and then fled below deck.

In between the realms, where the shadow met the night, Death waited for her daughters. The gloom surrounding her seethed, and the surrounding air snapped and shivered with a frosty tinge. Death paced, her bony jaw clenched, her eyes black and hollow and her every movement echoed with a faint sound of wailing, tiny pinpricks of malaise.

Then a bit of the shade parted and Bevire stepped through from another part of her sanctuary. Her shadows swirled to meet her mother's, and Death stopped moving. She slowly turned.

Bevire smiled and said, "Good morning, Mother."

"Good? What's good about it?" Death's voice rumbled through the enveloping space.

Bevire stepped back, surprised and anxious. "Why are you so upset? Did something go wrong?"

Death took a long breath, something moaning past the echo of the inhale. "Yes. No. Your brother is just stubborn." Her words seemed calmer, but she still glared. "He will not accept his destiny. Wants to protect the mortals first. When will he learn to stop this foolish obsession and embrace the darkness? He needs to take back this world!"

"He will never follow your version of his destiny. Your darkness. The past." Manume's voice drifted from another parted bit of the gloom, and a glowing Goddess of the Moon emerged from the inky black. "That is not why we came to help." She smiled and let her light fade as Death winced. "Hello, Mother."

"We came to save him, daughter." Death took a step forward. "Even from himself, if need be. He must come to Chaos. Restore the balance."

Manume shook her head. "No. That is not the way. He is different from the other son."

The words stopped Death cold, and she paused for a moment as if frozen in time. She stared, her eyes boring into Manume's, even as a confused Bevire asked, "What other son? What are you talking about?"

The eyes of Death and the Goddess of the Moon locked, a tug of force against madness, before the mother asked her daughter, "And what do you truly know of that? Of what happened?"

Manume shrugged. "More than I want. Little bird talked too much in his sleep. High in the trees, when he thought he was alone. I put the bits together. Eventually."

"What are you talking about?" An exasperated Bevire lashed out with the question, her shadows swirling.

Her sister glanced at her. "A secret. Tell you later if you promise to keep it." Bevire rolled her eyes but said nothing else.

Manume looked back at her mother. "I know. Nasty beast, that brother." A strange gasp came from Bevire, again ignored by the other two. "But he was all yours. All darkness. Not Morrannan. Morrannan is not all yours."

"Because he chose not to be mine! He chose the Light!

He chose the mortals!" Death's voice sliced the atmosphere like a knife and the air and shadows seemed to scream. Then, "He still does, but he can change his mind."

Manume sighed. "Oh, Mother. Mother. You never understood, did you? Who he truly is? Not Dark. Not Light. Not the God of Souls. He only calls himself that for his mortals. So they are not afraid. Like his family." She glanced over at Bevire, who cast her eyes downward, a look of guilt on her face. Then she shook her head, taking a step closer to her mother. "There were no choices. Just what is."

Death scowled, ignoring the exchange between sisters. "Ridiculous. Of course I understand. I know what my son is, what he can do."

Manume tilted her head, staring. "No, I don't think you do. No, you don't really know. Maybe in your head, but not your heart." Manume took a breath, her next words ringing clear and precise without a trace of madness. "He is more than the God of Souls. He is the bridge between Chaos and Harmony. He belongs to both realms, not one or the other. Free to walk where *he* wills, not you." She shifted her feet, her body swaying.

Death only glared.

"Mother is mad." Manume giggled. "I was mad once. Angry he did not do what I wanted. Recreate what I lost. But he understood better than I."

"I know all about your rift." Death snorted. "And I don't see the similarity. You had no spark left for creation. He had no choice in your circumstance. He has one in mine."

"No, Mother. I understood sparks. It was the other I refused to see. That sometimes you must accept that things end. Morrannan knows the truth of this." The Goddess of the Moon let out a soft sigh. "He can fix the realms, but not by bringing back what was. That is gone."

Death remained silent.

The Goddess of the Moon clucked her tongue. "You need to accept this, Mother," Manume chided, her tone full of disappointment. "He may die if you do not accept this. You cannot push him. Stubborn, stubborn brother."

"She's right." Bevire abruptly interjected into the conversation. "Trying to—to alter his destiny is a bad idea. I know. I tried." She sighed. "And I only managed to pull myself into the middle of this mess. Let it be, Mother. Let him handle his own life. Wherever it takes him."

Death looked at both her daughters, but addressed Bevire with the question, "Where does that leave me?"

Bevire laughed. "Oh, don't play the victim with me. We're too alike. You'll survive. And thrive. As soon as you stop feeling sorry for yourself."

Death took a step back, surprise flashing in her eyes and a frown on her lips. Manume giggled.

"Sister has a spine and some sense." The Goddess of the Moon whirled, scattering darkness in her wake.

"Stop that!" Death admonished her daughter. Manume stopped moving but still grinned widely. Death glared. "Fine. I'll leave him be. Let the consequences of that be on your heads."

Bevire rolled her eyes. "I think we can both live with that. We already have far worse things on our conscience."

Suddenly the Goddess of the Moon expelled a great heave of breath. "Yes. Many bad, bad things. Mother knows about bad things. Don't you, Mother?"

Death didn't answer.

Manume kept talking. "Did you tell him all the bad things? Or just what he needed to hear? Did he agree to go? Fly, fly on your dark wings to a sea that got lost? To fix what Grandfather broke? To bring a Crow to where he wants to be?"

Death turned a slightly lighter shade of pale, but replied, "He didn't. He's heading north again, to face a threat to his mortals. But he will get there all the same. I made sure of that. A small surprise woven in inky shadows."

Manume tilted her head. "Gifts in gifts?" Death nodded and the Moon Goddess frowned. "He won't like that."

A hiss from Bevire, and she asked, "What did you do?"

Death smiled, just a crack. "Took away his choice, if only in this. He will get where he needs to go if unhappily and reluctantly."

The Goddess of Shadows and Night sighed. "I suppose we must be satisfied with that. Everything else is prepared. The Grey Sisters and I are keeping a discreet eye on the Crow and we've arranged what you needed. It's ready." She managed a slight smile. "Is there anything else, or shall we go, then? I'd like to get back to Raven Rock."

"You can leave, sister. Mother and I need to discuss something else." Manume shot Bevire an odd look. "In private."

"What?" Bevire's tone was laced with irritation. "In my realm? You're dismissing me from my own sanctuary?"

"Yes." Manume ignored any objection. "Go now. Go, go, go."

Bevire scowled at her sister, but the Goddess of the Moon did not flinch, blink, or relent.

Finally, throwing up her hands, Bevire snapped, "Fine. I'll go. I'm sure the two of you can show yourselves out." In a flurry of pique and frustration she disappeared from her own sanctuary in a swirl of shadow.

After Bevire left, Manume softly asked her mother, "Why did you go to the Rock Island Temple?"

Surprised, Death asked in return, "Are you spying on me?"

Manume smiled. "No, but the Grey Sisters are. Father

asked them to watch you. And rightly so, I think." She giggled. "Now answer the question. Why did you go to the Rock Island Temple before you met with Morrannan?"

Death turned her head away, but the Goddess of the Moon still heard the words she spoke. "I went to see the Oracle. To seek her help in bringing your brother to the darkness."

Manume sighed. "How did *that* go?"

"The little slip of a girl laughed at me. Said neither of us had a say in my son's destiny." Death turned to face her daughter. "That Oracle looked me in the eye without one trace of fear and told me to gather the pieces of my past and make my peace. That the future was set on a different path and it couldn't be altered."

"*Ooooh.* Naughty girl. Telling off Mother." Manume giggled. "Is she still alive?"

"Yes." Death hissed the word. "I restrained myself."

"Good Mother." Manume tilted her head. "She is not wrong, though. You cannot control his destiny. Only protect him."

Death sighed, and an echoing loss and grief a thousandfold dripped into the air. "I miss it. What it was before Ulerne. Before the Light. I miss walking the world, instead of the corner left to me by circumstance."

"Are you unhappy? Is Mother sad?" The Moon Goddess took a step forward, concern on her face.

"No. Yes. I don't know." Death sighed again. "I am... discontent, I am..." Her voice faded away and the air grew cold.

"Lonely?" Manume reached out and brushed the edge of her mother's cloak. Blackness shifted and the air rumbled.

"Perhaps," came the faint reply.

"You can come visit me. The Archipelago misses you.

The creatures there miss you. They tried to talk to me when I came." She sniffed. "It did not go well. Apparently I confused them. They only came because I was a part of you. They smelled it in me." She scrunched her nose. "I think that is why they like Hugh. He is dead. Part of you." Manume craned her neck and leaned her head sideways to see her mother's face. "You could walk the world again. At least my corner of it."

Death shifted space at her words and an overwhelming silence enveloped their murky surroundings. It hung like the air before a storm: oppressive, heavy and thick with the potential onslaught of a primeval force. Time stilled and movement ceased. There remained only Death and the Moon, watching each other, waiting for the truth to be acknowledged. Finally Death inhaled. A slight breath, but one that shifted destiny.

She smiled and said, "I would like that."

Manume smiled back. "Good. Wait until you meet Hugh."

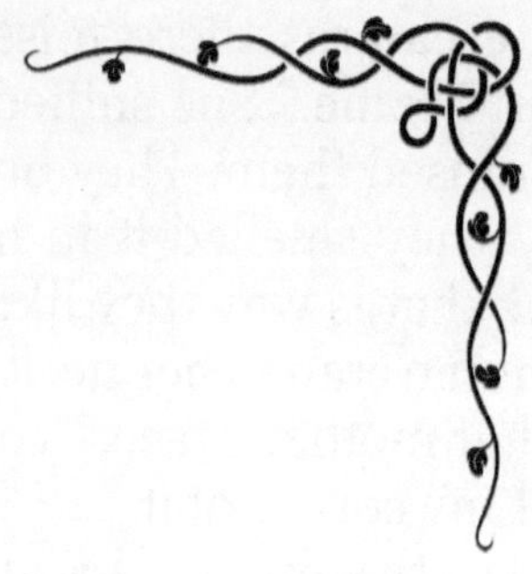

Chapter Eleven
Stallion Bay

The three pirate ships drifted off the coast of Stallion Bay, hidden by a spit of land that formed the inlet. Twilight slowly faded into night and above them the first twinkling of stars began to form. Black Axe Morgan stood on the prow of his ship, staring at the island, waiting for the right moment to come. Above his head the Crow perched precariously on a sail rigging.

Morgan glanced up and grinned wide. "Look at this place. She's a beautiful isle, Breakwater Key. Wild horses, grassy plains, lovely women. Used to have a friend of sorts that lived here. Not in the Stallion Bay port, mind, but in a town on the opposite side called Seven Rock. Wonder if she's still living there or even still living?" Morgan gave a grunt. "Might be an old woman now, looking out at the sea same as us, under the stars same as us."

"Perhaps," the Crow replied and ruffled his feathers against the wind. "You mortals have odd life spans. But you know nothing of the stars."

"Really?" Morgan glanced up again, this time with a sneer. "I spent most of me life sailing under or by the stars, birdie. I think I know a thing or two."

The Crow made a sound like a sniff. "Those tiny pinpricks of light you call stars are mere minuscule glimpses of the real thing. You know nothing of their majesty, their fire, their power. Their magic." The Crow puffed a breath and a wheeze of regret. "Their light sings to your blood, urging you to dance in their radiance, to dive against their edges and even fall into their fire. I have flown the pathways among the stars, seen them close in all their intensity, and dared to snatch a drop of their purity to hold as my own."

"You stole a star?" Morgan's voice held a note of incredulity.

The Crow nodded. "A beautiful keepsake." He sighed. "Until I came back here. There, in my home, in my heart, it was a piece of a star. Here it was only a power stone."

"Was?" Morgan caught the past tense. "It's gone? Destroyed?"

"Not gone. Just lost to me. I tried to barter with it. I was cheated and the star taken from me. So much has been taken from me."

"Poor birdie." Despite the words, Morgan sounded more amused than sympathetic. "Too bad, would've liked to seen a bit of a star. Or even a power stone. Tried to steal one of those once, something called Wayfarer's Lament. The gent that had it turned out to be too much of a tricky sort and gave me the slip before I pilfered it."

The Crow chuckled. "A good thing for you he did. The Wayfarer's Lament is a dark thing that feeds on wicked mortals like you. It would have most likely sucked the life out of you slowly. As it most likely did to the wretch who kept it from you."

Morgan blinked and sucked in a slight breath. "Good thing I didn't steal it, then. Don't sound like a pleasant way to leave this world. Must've been a sick bastard that conjured up that bit of rock."

Another chuckle from the Crow. "It certainly isn't a quick way to die. Most excruciating, in fact. And it wasn't conjured. It's all that's left of a particularly nasty beast that lived a very long time ago."

Morgan shook his head. "You do know some odd things, birdie, indeed you do." A sudden flash of light caught his attention and he smiled. "There's the beacon light. Time to sail, boys!" He shouted the last words to his crew, and a flurry of movement happened behind him as the men prepared and the other ships were signalled. The trio of ships lurched forward, steering towards the light. Morgan's face lit up in wicked joy. "Steady now, steady," he whispered. "Follow the channel, use the light to steer."

The ships sailed around the cove flawlessly, running dark, using the old charted pirate route, avoiding the beacon's illumination directly but using its light as navigation. The three vessels slipped in to Stallion Bay harbour silently and undetected, coming into range and position. Then they slowly turned broadside into a semi-circle, formed a barricade line and readied their deck guns.

Then Morgan shouted the order, "Fire the cannon, boys! I want those guns blazing!"

Within moments, the lanterns were lit, the pirate flags raised high, and the weapons discharged with a boom and rattling recoils across the deck. Cannon shots whizzed through the air in rapid succession as the ships bombarded the Stallion Bay port. Flying ammunition smashed into the sea wall and piers, dockside taverns and berthed ships. Wood splintered with a crunch as metal shot ripped through the wharves while screams and shouts rang out amidst the booming reverberation of cannon fire. In the flickering light of the beacon and docks, Morgan spied a flurry of people fleeing for their lives. No answering weapon's fire boomed out from the port, and Morgan smiled. He had been right, catching them unawares. Stallion Bay put up no defence.

He shouted another order. "Keep up the assault, boys! I'll send the signal for the next step in the plan!"

From the prow of the *Shadow Raider*, amid the continued destructive barrage, Morgan tossed a burst of green flame into the night sky. Within minutes, longboats full of men were lowered from the ocean-facing side of the ships, ready to invade the town. As soon as they touched water, the longboats rowed to shore alongside the onslaught, muscles straining against the oars, curses and prayers muttered to protect against the death flying through the air. Finn sat in the back of the lead boat, face grinning, rowing like a madman. They landed on the shore past the docks, out of range of the cannon fire, and hauled their boats past the tide mark. Then they waited.

On board his ship, Morgan watched their journey, chuckling as they arrived safely and established their position. He sent up another magic signal and the cannon fire slowly halted. Another signal and his pirates rushed the port.

Their attack and invasion met little resistance and Morgan watched it all through the spyglass as his men cut down docked sailors, the harbourmaster and the harbour crew, those poor souls too afraid to run. Then one last signal and Morgan's ships manoeuvred slowly around, swinging direction on creaks and groans of wood. The manoeuver happened on shallow breath and wicked grins until they came into position. Then the vessels sailed into dock at what was left of the wharves. Morgan's pirates guided the vessels into damaged berths with the help of their fellows, and the remainder of his men disembarked.

"Welcome to Stallion Bay, boys! Go pick their pockets clean and leave any opposition for the boneyard." Morgan laughed and drew his sword, striding across the broken and battered port. He headed into the town proper with Finn at his heels and emerald flames glowing around his torso, while, overhead, the Crow trailed him. The rest of his men chased his path with raucous cries and whoops of accepted victory, lanterns and weapons swinging from their clenched fingers.

They met deserted streets as frightened and confused townsfolk cowered in their homes. Morgan's men kicked in the doors of random houses as they marched, looting and killing wantonly. They filled pockets and satchels with coin, food, and other valuables, dragged bodies into the streets, hauled screaming victims from their dwellings to gut them in the roadways and splatter the town with blood. A few brave people fought back, but most fell under the pirate swords without a struggle.

They hacked a swath of death through the town mostly unopposed until they reached the marketplace. As they emerged into the open space, the illumination from Morgan and the lanterns showed dozens of angry and armed men and women lined up to stop their invasion. Morgan signalled a halt to his company and laughed.

"So the sheep show some teeth to the wolves, do they?"

"Aye." A woman dressed in a blue tunic and trousers stepped forward, carrying a sword like she knew how to use it. She raised it at an angle to her body in a solid grip, not awkward or hesitant. She took a defensive position and snapped defiantly, "Do your worst!" Behind her more weapons were raised.

Morgan laughed again, deep and long and from the

belly. He sprouted a wicked grin and replied, "You don't want my worst, poppet. You'd be screaming for all sorts of reasons, none of them good or pleasurable." He took a step forward and clicked the tip of her blade with his own before withdrawing. "But I like your spirit and I'm in a fine mood. Lower your weapons and I'll give your people an hour to evacuate the town. I'll allow you all to retreat to the hills. Let us have the town and we won't massacre the lot of you."

She raised her chin. "And if we refuse?"

Morgan held up his other hand and danced flames from his fingers. He thrust his hand forward and let her feel the seething edge of the energy. She shrank back, her sword wavering and then lowering. As if on attached strings, the other townsfolk lowered their weapons as well.

Morgan sheathed his sword, noticing his men shooting him grumbles and dirty looks. Not one lowered or sheathed their weapons. He cocked his head. "What's your name, lass?"

The woman bit her lip, but replied, "Anne Brennan."

Morgan smiled. Then he punched the woman in the face and shouted, "Kill them all, boys! Not one left alive!" He punched Anne again, shouting, "Never trust a lying pirate," and then again, knocking her unconscious. He scooped up her limp form and slung it over his shoulder, watching his pirates make short work of the would-be defenders.

"Finn!" The youth whirled as Morgan called, smearing blood across his cheek with a hand. "You have command of this rabble for the moment! Loot the town and kill who you like! I'm taking this prize back to the ship." He smacked the unconscious Anne's backside. "Then I'll return and help raze this town!"

With a grunt he turned around and walked through

town towards the port, heaving and sweating under his burden.

At the dock, he threw Anne on the ground amidst some rubble and took a few deep inhales, trying to catch his breath. He heard the rustle of wings, and the Crow asked, "Not as young as you used to be?"

Morgan looked up and glared. "You try toting a hundred plus pounds of dead weight through a town. It ain't easy."

"Then why take her? Why not just kill her?" The Crow's voice sounded genuinely confused.

"Like I said, I admire her spirit. It'll be fun breaking that spirit." Scurrying feet made him glance towards his ships, but he saw only two of his pirates rushing forward.

He grinned. "You two scallywags step lively and haul this prisoner on to the *Shadow Raider* and lock her in my brig!" Morgan kicked Anne in the hip, rolling her over, and the two pirates started dragging her away. Morgan yelled after them, "See she stays isolated and locked up tight! No one touches her! She's mine now! No one else's!"

Morning found Morgan leaning against the wall of his brig, ogling a still-defiant Anne, who glared at him through cell bars. He grinned and asked, "You enjoy spending the night on my ship? Not that it matters, seeing as you've no say in your accommodations. I'm in control of your life now, missy."

"No one is in control of me!" Anne spat at him, the spittle landing far short of his boots.

Morgan laughed. "You're so wrong about that, girlie." He plucked a coin from his pocket and flipped it, catching it in mid-air. "Know where I got this? From that red house on the north hill. I think you know the one." Morgan chuckled as he watched the colour and the fire drain from her face.

"Loved the painting that hung opposite the fireplace. Nice family portrait, it was." Morgan grinned at Anne's sharp intake of breath, and he turned his head, gesturing to men standing beyond Anne's range of vision.

"Bring him in, boys. Let her get a good look at what I done. And make sure to bring them shackles for after."

Three men slowly shambled forward, dragging a large, misshapen object carelessly wrapped in a red-stained sheet. Anne whimpered as the pirates dropped it in front of the cell.

"Take the cloth off, boys, let her see."

The three men tugged and yanked, tearing away the cloth to reveal a mutilated corpse. The face remained untouched, but the body was missing an arm and a foot, guts hung from his stomach and chunks of flesh had been cut away from the torso. Anne screamed and retched, turning away to vomit.

"Hard ain't it, seeing a loved one dead?" Morgan snickered and sniffed, waving a hand against the stench now coming from her cell. "Always a shock. Especially with it being your brother." Morgan advanced on the cell, bent down and grabbed Anne's arm through the bars, jerking her body forward. A trail of spit and bile dribbled down her chin and she whimpered.

He slammed her crying, shocked face against the cell door. He leaned in close, his fetid breath puffing against her skin, and whispered, "He was alive when I did all those things. Cut off his parts, sliced open his guts. He was strong, but he begged in the end. Begged me to end him quick. I didn't. I let him die slow and in agony." He let go of her arm and added, "So who is in control now, girlie?"

He rose and stepped away, turning to his men. "Bring her out of that there cell in shackles, so she can see the rest."

The men unlocked the cell, shackled Anne, and handed her over to Morgan. She didn't struggle or try to escape. She complied meekly, her eyes locked on her brother's body. Morgan pushed her forward, shouting over his shoulder, "Rewrap the body and toss it overboard into the harbour."

That roused Anne, who twisted in Morgan's grip, shrieking, "No, you can't! He needs to be buried, he needs—" A backhand slap from Morgan across her mouth stopped her shouts and drove her to her knees.

"Don't tell me what I have to do!" Morgan yanked her to her feet and slapped her again. "You got no say in nothing anymore! Shut your trap and keep it shut!" He shoved her forward and kept shoving until they were both on deck. Anne remained silent, her body shaking until Morgan hauled her to the prow of his ship to show her the docks of Stallion Bay. She let out a cry of horror and disbelief.

Sitting on the wharves, on top of barrels and crates, and swinging in the rigging of a half-sunken ship at dock, were the severed heads of the citizens of Stallion Bay. As Anne stared, another whimper slipped out. "What did you do? My neighbours, my friends. What did you do?"

"Killed them, poppet. Some slipped away, but I got most of them. Then we looted the town, taking your coin and anything else we fancied. I even got two more ships for me fleet." Morgan turned her head with his hands and she saw four other ships anchored in the harbour flying crude Sword and Skull flags from their mast. "All in all it was a most successful visit. I even got to leave me mark and redecorate." He laughed as he pushed Anne's face back to stare at the heads and the ruins of Stallion Bay.

Morgan leaned closer, wrapping an arm around her and whispering in her ear, "Say bye-bye to the place, poppet. You ain't ever going to see it again. This ship's your home now." He suddenly whirled around and yanked at her arm, pulling her with him as he strode across the deck. "Now it's back to the brig with you, girlie! And the rest of you scallywags, step lively and set sail! We got places to be and ports to plunder!"

Echoes of his laughter wafted over the deck as he dragged a now screaming Anne back below decks, to the brig. Perched on a mast's crossbeam, the Crow watched him go and cawed a note of distaste.

"Such a wretch you are, pirate." The whisper vanished in the wind. "This is what I am reduced to, consorting with the likes of you." The Crow turned his head, staring out to sea. "In the old days I would have pecked out your eyes and feasted on your bones while you screamed for mercy." A sigh escaped his beak. "And now…" Another sigh. "Soon it will be over. Soon he will come and I will take the power of the God of Souls." The Crow glanced back. Morgan stood on the lower deck, having handed off Anne to crew members. "Perhaps I'll take your magic as well, pirate. Do these mortals one last favour before I go."

The Crow ruffled his feathers, pleased at the thought of double-crossing Morgan. He turned back to the sea, feeling a sense of satisfaction.

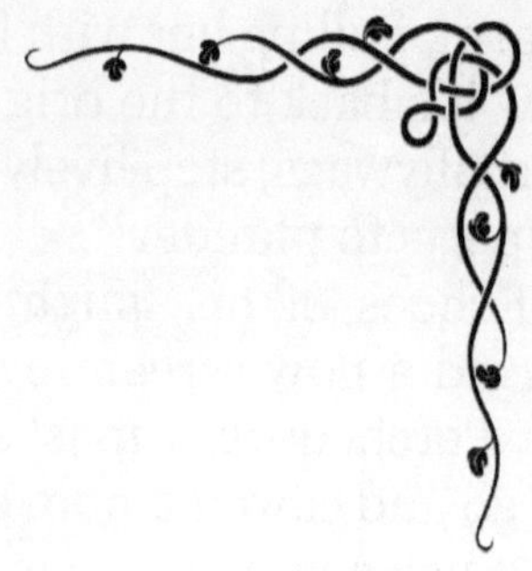

Chapter Twelve
Battles at Sea

Morgan and his fleet rounded the island of Breakwater Key, headed to Spitfire Reef and their next pillaging port of call. From the quarterdeck Morgan watched the horizon retreat in their wake, whistling an off-key tune, when a cry rang out from the spotters in the rigging.

"Navy! It's the bloody Navy of the Royal Court. Heading our way through the channel!"

Morgan snatched up a spyglass, shouting, "How many ships?"

"A dozen at least," came the reply.

As he raised the spyglass, he muttered, "Damnable navy. Always trying to spoil the fun." He scanned the horizon and spotted the ships—at full sail and moving fast—barrelling straight at his tiny fleet. He also spotted something else. A figure in the water swimming alongside the ships and keeping pace. "Damnation! It's the bloody Sea Goddess! Why in of the dark depths is she with the navy?"

He snapped the spyglass shut as a shiver of anger and disgust ran along his skin. "Hard about, lads! We ain't equipped to tangle with the Sea Goddess! We need to turn tail and run! Signal the other ships and head to more open water!"

The crew jumped to obey, shifting course, trimming sail and waving the signal flags to warn their companions on the other vessels. Morgan swiftly crossed to the front of the quarterdeck shouting, "Faster, lads! Bring her about faster! So I can buy us time to escape." He glanced at the stern, muttering, "We need to be out there. It's too confined between these islands."

No sooner did the words escape his mouth, then the waters rolled, tossing the ships from their course, and a towering, rushing wave stormed across the sea. The monstrous wall of water headed straight at Morgan's fleet, threatening to swamp the vessels. Before he could react, shadows formed in the air between the pirates and the wave, ahead of the turning fleet. Abruptly they solidified and the onrushing water smashed into the barrier. The shadow wall crumbled but the momentum of the water halted, the liquid cascading back into the sea.

Above his head Morgan heard a caw and looked up to see the Crow flying back to the *Shadow Raider*. He whispered, "Good job, birdie. Good job." He snatched up the spyglass again and trained it on the fast-approaching navy ships and Lynna. As he watched, he heard the flap of wings, and the shape of the Crow swooped past to land on the rail.

"What are you planning to do, Captain? I can't hold her off forever." The voice of the Crow hit Morgan's ears over the sound of the crashing sea. "Neither can you. Not at sea. In very sinkable ships. It won't be long before she figures out to come at us from underneath."

"Don't I know it! Damnable gods! Always interfering!" He snapped the spyglass shut and glared at the Crow. "At least she's backed off. Your trick probably spooked her."

"She won't stay spooked for long." The Crow shifted position. "And those navy ships are gaining on us."

"We just need to buy time. Get out to more open water, and out from between these islands so I can do my trick." Morgan clenched his jaw against the looming spectre of the navy. "We ain't turning fast enough. That goddess slowed us down with her waves."

The Crow tilted his head. "Perhaps we need a distraction. Something to deflect their attention and gain us time." He stretched his wings. "Have any tricks in that stolen magic you're so proud of?"

"What about your tricks?" Morgan spat and scowled, heart pounding as he stared into the sea, watching it swirl as the ship banked. He glanced towards the incoming navy, scanning for the Sea Goddess under the water. He saw no sign of her presence, but a smaller shadow flitted under the surface and he suddenly grinned.

"Birdie! They're still razorfish in these waters?"

A puzzled Crow replied, "Yes. Swarms of them."

"Then that should serve well enough." Morgan turned to Finn. "Bring me our prisoner! Haul her up here in shackles and be quick about it!"

Morgan leaned over the rail, eyes locked on the view of the gaining navy ships and the Sea Goddess, now close enough to see without a spyglass. He saw his ships coming broadside around the turn, and flirted with the idea of cannon fire, but without the range, it was wasted ammunition. He also saw, in the distance, the sea around the goddess began to churn.

Morgan scowled. "Maybe I should fire on you."

Commotion on deck and feminine screams brought

his attention back to the ship. Finn and two other crewmen dragged a violently struggling Anne up to the quarterdeck.

"About time!" Morgan snapped and strode to meet the quartet. "That damn goddess is fixing to attack again." As he skidded to a stop in front of Anne and her captors, he backhanded her across the mouth, cutting off her screams. Blood trickled from the corner of her mouth as she yanked against the grip of the men who held her. Morgan smacked her again and Anne spat at him. Snarling at her spirited resistance, Morgan punched her several times in the head and face until she stopped struggling.

"Let her go, boys."

His boys took their hands away and Anne dropped to her knees, dazed and clearly in pain. She retched and tried to crawl away before Morgan yanked her arm and pulled her to her feet. He dragged her, stumbling, to the stern rail and drew his dagger.

"Sorry about this, poppet, but it's you or me. Would've liked to kept ya around longer and all, but this is the end of our fun." Morgan stabbed her in the shoulder and then sliced a deep gash in her leg. She screeched in pain and her blood flowed freely. He dropped the dagger and glanced out at the goddess. The sea around her foamed and rose in a wave.

Morgan yelled, "Time to choose, goddess." Green energy sizzled from his body and he lifted Anne like a rag doll, throwing her from the ship in a superhuman effort. She rose on a tide of his emerald magic, her terrified shrieks shattering the air, and Morgan guided her straight into the sea with barely a splash. She sank like a stone, weighted down by her iron shackles and pushed by the last wave of Morgan's magic. As the ocean swallowed Anne, Lynna's wave dissipated and she dove to rescue the woman.

Above his head, the Crow remarked, "That won't

distract the goddess for long."

"Wait for it, birdie." Morgan grinned. Moments after his words, the sea hummed with life, dark forms swimming a beeline for the two submerged women. Morgan chuckled. "There they are. Razorfish. Those things will scent blood from a mile off. I knew they'd come. The goddess will have her hands full holding them off if she wants to save my Anne. Blood drives them mad. They'll try to tear 'em both to pieces."

Despite Morgan's magic, Anne hit the water hard, in a bruise-inducing plummet that drove her far beneath the surface of the sea. Blood streamed from stab wounds and into the surrounding water. Through the pain, she struggled and thrashed, weighed down by irons, desperately trying to swim and not swallow seawater. Her lungs burned as she held her breath, bleeding, sinking, inching closer to death in a span of moments. Then, inexplicably, she felt a hand on her waist and her body rising to the surface; she realized the Goddess of the Sea was plucking her from her doom. Anne gulped air as her head broke past the water, but relief was only momentary; a swarm of razorfish was bearing down on them, jaws snapping.

Anne screamed and Lynna wrapped her arms about the woman, spinning a whirlpool around the two of them. Shouts from the navy ships echoed in the air, punctuated by the fleeting sound of booming cannons. The smell of smoke mixed with the scent of blood as crazed razorfish leapt into the swirling mass of water Lynna created.

Anne struggled in Lynna's grasp, shrieking as dozens of jaws gnashed against the edge of their whirlpool cocoon. She felt the water rise, forming a spout, and rotate ever faster, fish thrown off in all directions as the Goddess of the Sea fashioned their escape. Across the sea they travelled in a gyrating waterspout to fling themselves over the rail of Pelham's waiting ship.

The pair tumbled to the deck, rolling, until they came to a painful halt, smacking against the foremast. Lynna grunted, but Anne gave no sound, all her screams and cries spent in the sea.

Lynna pulled herself to one knee, Anne still clinging to her, shaking in her arms. Blood covered both of them and Lynna shouted, "She's hurt! We need help."

Two navy sailors rushed to their aid, prying Anne from the Sea Goddess and trying to staunch her bleeding. Another ran to fetch the ship's doctor from below decks, while yet another handed Lynna his coat. She donned it out of respect, if with slight distaste, for the men she now called friends. Lynna looked up and caught Pelham's eye as he barked orders from the quarterdeck. He nodded and gave her a quick smile. Lynna moved forward, making her way to join him, glancing back to ensure Anne had the care she needed. Then she bounded up the steps to the upper deck.

"How is she?" Pelham asked as Lynna came to his side.

"Not dead. Hopefully your men can keep her alive." Lynna curled her lip in a snarl. "He cut her. Deep." She took a breath. "Did the bastard pirate get away?"

"Not yet, though they turned their ships and are trying to flee. It will be a race, but we have the faster ships. We'll catch them."

Lynna went to the rail and leaned over, craning her neck to get a view towards the prow. *Star's Hope* led the charge, and she tightened her fingers over the wood in eager anticipation as she saw the gap closing between the pirates and the navy.

"We're coming for you, you bastard. And by the shoals I'll drag you to the depths myself and drown the last breath from your lungs."

Morgan stood on the quarterdeck in a wide-legged stance, glowering at the gaining navy ships and screaming at his crew. "Faster, you bastards, faster! Get them sails trim! I need more speed! Or by my blade, I'll toss a few of you overboard to lessen the weight!"

A few terrified expressions blossomed on the crew as they strained at ropes, grunted and uttered curses, putting their backs into their duties. Morgan cast an angry glance back at his men before returning his gaze to the navy.

"Where is this trick of yours?" To his left, the voice of the Crow drifted to Morgan's ears. "This bit of magic that will save us all?"

"It's coming. I do it here, this close to the islands, things might get messy. We just have to stay ahead of them 'til we get far enough into open waters."

"Captain!" A sudden cry of alarm shouted down from the rigging. "We got more trouble coming in! Another ship sailing full tilt towards us, in from the sea! They're trying to box us in!"

"What?" Morgan whirled, racing down the steps to the lower deck. He sprinted the length of the deck to the prow, yanked a spyglass from his coat pocket and aimed it at the sea's horizon. Sure enough he spotted a ship. A familiar ship. Before them, bearing down on his pirate fleet, was the *Celestial Jewel.*

Morgan screamed, a sound of triumph and rage, shouting, "It's the bloody God of Souls at last!" He danced a mad jig on the prow, screeching with joy. "By the shoals, my luck has turned!" He swivelled to face his crew, a manic grin plastered on his face. "It's time for glory! We're going in, guns ablazing! Prepare for battle! We'll blast that damn ship out of the water!"

He raced back the length of the ship laughing like a madman. Returning to the quarterdeck he shouted at the helm, "Steer us straight towards that damn *Celestial Jewel!* We'll show Captain Morrow our guns, by the shoals, and sink his ship!" Then he yelled more orders to the helm and the crew on the lower deck. "Close as you can, and then turn her broadside to starboard! Trim the sail and get us more speed! And I want those port side deck cannons ready to fire at that ship! With any luck we'll hit straight over the bow before they can turn. Signal the damned rest of this fleet to do the same!"

A frightened cry rose, "What about the navy?"

"Forget the blasted navy! We're hunting a god today!" Morgan roared and his men quaked. "'Sides, we're headed away from those navy bastards! Naught to worry yet!"

The crew jumped to obey Morgan's orders and the deck vibrated as the *Shadow Raider* trimmed sails and picked up speed. The Crow took to the air, flying along the edge of the ship for a better view, before returning to the quarterdeck.

He landed on the rail, his chuckle echoing across the boards. "He has come!" The bird flapped his wings in excitement. "This could be our chance."

"Aye! He's ours. Come right to his bloody death, birdie. Right to his bloody death."

***

"Pirates coming in, sir!" The shout came down from the crow's nest of the *Celestial Jewel.* "Looks like they may be trying a raking manoeuvre!"

"Aye! Bring her about, starboard turn, Mr. Anders!" Rafe barked the order to the helm and shouted more commands to the lower deck. "Furl the lower sails and prepare her for battle! Keep an eye to the other ships! Watch for doubling! We don't want them firing from both sides! And send word to the gunners. Prepare to fire the cannons."

The crew jumped to duty, sails lowered, the ship groaning in the turn. A man ran below deck to relay the order to the gunners and the creak of the wheels of the metal cannons soon echoed. The *Jewel* pushed ahead, the sea slapping against her hull, drawing close enough to see the billowing sails and the gleaming metal of the pirate guns, sailing right into firing range. Shouts of the crew and the clank of the ship echoed, every muscle tensed and jaw clenched until the boom of cannon fire thundered from Morgan's ship.

First shot went to the pirates, but fell short into the sea.

Rafe smiled. He shouted, "Fire when ready!" and the echo of the order relayed down below. Then the crack and reverberation of the *Jewel*'s cannons shattered across the sea and multiple shots buzzed along the air. Some went wide, one battered a still turning ship—smashing away the top of its figurehead—and yet another clipped a mast of Morgan's vessel before speeding over the deck into the water.

"We have the better guns, boys! Blast those pirates out of the water! We'll send Black Axe Morgan straight to the bottom of the sea!"

A cheer rose from the crew, only to be strangled on the wind as the ship shuddered violently.

Rafe grabbed the rail, and a quiver danced under his hand. "Have we been hit? Is it an ambush?"

Only cries of confusion answered him as another shudder tore through his vessel and a strange dark glow rippled over the decks and twisted up the masts and sails. The crew yelped as tingles sparked off their skin.

"What the bloody hell!" came the cry from Anders,

now struggling with the wheel that developed a mind of its own. "The ship's fighting me. She's gone mad."

Swaying with the rumble of the deck, and feeling a surge of raw power not his own, Rafe replied, dread in his voice, "It's not the ship. It's something else in control."

The boom of the ship's cannons echoed his words and the air wafted with the smell of smoke. A chill ran through him.

"Cease firing! Send the order down! Stop the guns!"

"Sir!" Blackthorne's concern shouted over the roar of battle. "That'll leave us defenceless! The pirates!"

"Do it! Now!" Rafe saw a man dash below decks and the guns of the *Jewel* silenced. "And pray we survive this."

With his words the ship heaved into a starboard turn, nearly listing as it banked. The sea rose in great waves, forming a shining wall of water that encircled the *Jewel*. Energy snapped between drops of salty liquid, black and inky, snaking around and around the ship.

Through the misty barrier Rafe saw the pirate ships gain ground and blast their cannons at them. He watched the crew flinch and scramble for cover. The shot hurled forward to smack the barrier and fall, dropping harmlessly into the ocean.

The *Jewel* survived blast after cannon blast, each shot and round futilely striking against the magic shield until the ship came about and barrelled straight out to sea. The deck vibrated and glimmered in coal-black sparks and wisps of energy. Ahead of them the air and sea opened in a gaping obsidian hole: a portal leading into a void.

Rafe stared at it as the crew screamed and the ship sailed full tilt into its maw. He saw Anders still wrestling with the wheel, heard Blackthorne shouting useless orders and Mouse's terrified shrieks.

He took a breath, waited, and in that instant, the portal

swallowed the *Celestial Jewel.*

"Bloody hell! What the damnation just happened! Blasted coward turned tail!" Morgan whirled on the Crow, who had pulled in his wings, almost seeming to shrink into himself. "What was that! And how do we follow the bastard?"

"You don't." The Crow said the words quietly, with something akin to fear. "That was her magic. Not his."

"Her? Who the blazes are you—"

"Captain! The navy's still coming!" Finn's voice broke past Morgan's query. "What do we do?"

"Blast!" He snarled at the Crow as he turned. "This ain't over. You'll explain what's going on after."

Morgan raced to the back of the stern and scanned the horizon, cursing the pursuing navy ships. "Blast it all, can't they leave a man alone!" He curled his lip and made up his mind. "We're in position, at least." He turned back and shouted, "Signal the other ships! Full sail and close ranks! I want to be to able see the ugly faces of the other crews as we sail! We're getting the damnation out of here!"

Morgan waited as his orders were carried out, and sidled up to the Crow. "You wanted to see my trick, birdie. Well, it's coming."

The Crow tilted his head. "Let's hope it goes better than our encounter with the God of Souls."

"Aye." Morgan scowled. "Damn it, I almost had the bastard!" He curled his hand into a fist. "I almost had him."

"Another day." The Crow clacked his beak. "Now work your magic and get us away from these navy ships, please. I still have need of you and have no wish to see you hang." The Crow flapped his wings, thinking to himself, *Not yet at least.* He flew into the air, circling before landing on a sail crossbar.

Morgan growled and spat, but moved to the far railing at the stern. He checked the distance from land, finally satisfied. He summoned his power and tossed five orbs of green energy into the air one by one. Then he cast the orbs out across the sea where they settled lightly in the water.

Morgan took a breath and whispered, *"Dreswych iddan."*

A flash of emerald broke across the surface of the sea and ghostly images rose on the wave of illumination, phantoms of the fleeing pirates.

"Illusion? That's your grand trick?" The Crow dripped sarcasm from his perch.

"Nah. That's just to confuse them whilst I prepare the rest." Morgan looked up, grinning.

The Crow glanced at the water. The navy ships did seem to be slowing. He looked down at Morgan.

The pirate had closed his eyes and repeatedly chanted one word softly, *"Danabyth."*

The Crow moved his gaze back out to sea, watching the illusion of ships. As Morgan murmured his spell they began to glow, brighter and fiercer, building in intensity until...

"Here it comes, birdie." Morgan's voice held a chuckle, and then he shouted, "Full sail and speed! Signal the other ships! We're getting out of here, boys!"

The Crow stared, fascinated as the chimera of an emerald fleet burst into magical flame, erupted in a tremendous surge that smashed towards the navy fleet and backwashed against the pirate vessels. In that instant the Crow seized his chance.

As the spell exploded across the stern and the sea, the Crow swooped down from the mast, his wings outstretched and his head bowed. He flew towards the deck, along the edge of the magic, and quickly snatched a fragment of emerald energy, swallowing it whole. He settled onto the rail and watched Morgan, but the pirate did not remark on what he did. The Crow folded his wings and watched Morgan's conjuring do its work.

The pirate fleet picked up speed, fuelled by wind and magic, sailing away from the once-pursuing navy, who now battled rough choppy waters and the brunt of an undulation of magical energy. The navy could do nothing to chase the enemy, their full attention on not capsizing and trying to survive any damage to their ships. The pirate fleet soon left them behind, heading around Spitfire Reef and to freedom.

As the navy faded into the distance, Morgan gave the Crow a glare. "Told you I could get us gone, birdie. And well I did."

The Crow only flexed his wings, a small bit of green magic tickling the back of his throat.

Chapter Thirteen
Shanghaied

As the *Celestial Jewel* entered the portal from the seas, the ship and crew shuddered, shock and fear awash on deck. Instead of sky and clouds above their heads they saw black undulating mist, and they travelled not on waters but through flowing, snapping rivulets of energy and red-coloured magic.

Anders remained at the helm even though he had no control and the wheel moved of its own accord. Other crew clung to rigging, the gunwale or masts, while others huddled on deck, pressed against the gunwale or the sides of the ship. Rafe stared at the dark horizon until a hand fell on his shoulder.

Blackthorne's trembling voice asked, "What's going on, sir? What's happened?"

"We've been shanghaied, Blackthorne. By my mother. Damn her dark heart. Only thing to do is ride it out and find the source of it." Rafe pulled away and marched from the quarterdeck.

He dashed below decks, summoning his own power, his senses open to his mother's interference, and traced her trail of magic straight to his quarters. He burst through the door, his eyes and skin snapping with blue energy, and came to a dead halt. Above his desk floated a map. The map of the Lost Sea given to him as a gift. From the vellum and ink, sparks snapped and black smoky tendrils snaked out, tethering themselves to the wood of the ship. The boards under his feet shuddered.

"Damn her! It was a bloody snare and I tumbled in!"

As he ground his teeth and balled his fingers into fists, Rafe heard the pounding of running feet behind him and then the shout, "What in all the islands!" He turned to see Pinky Jasper and several more of his crew standing in the corridor, staring through the open doorway.

"Don't come in, men!" Rafe snapped.

"Never crossed my mind, sir," Pinky replied, fear in his voice. "Blackthorne sent us to help, but I don't know what good we'll be against a—a flying magical map! By the shoals, that's a new one, even for us."

Rafe nearly smiled, despite everything. "There's nothing any of us can do, Mr. Jasper. That's my mother's magic and she's controlling the ship now." Rafe gritted his teeth. "Go back up on deck and inform the crew to stay on alert and keep the ship tacked and ready. We're going into the Lost Sea whether we wish to or not, and no telling what's waiting on the other side." Seeing the petrified looks on his crew's faces, he added, "And tell them we're in no immediate danger. Not sure what we'll be facing when we depart this place, but we're safe enough for the journey."

With an "aye, sir" Pinky and the other men left Rafe and headed back above deck.

Rafe moved cautiously into the room, sliding around his desk and slipping the diary out of a top drawer. Black sparks snapped around him and he felt an answering unease roll up from the bowels of the ship. He put a hand on a wall of his quarters.

He whispered to the ship, "I know. I don't like it either. But we can't fight it, not without things getting messy. We have to let her take us through the cracks and into the Lost Sea. To whatever awaits us."

Still, his mother's treachery rankled. Sending him a spelled map to make certain he did her bidding. He wanted to scream his fury to the world.

"Damn her." He smacked his palm on the wall, wincing at the sting. He glared at the map, wishing he could tear the thing to pieces. Frustration and resentment chased each other around his mind.

And yet, part of him admired the spell itself. It was not simple to open a magic conduit between places, let alone send a ship and her crew through in the blink of an eye. He had thought the extent of conduit travel to be limited to a few souls or gods, as with his portals or the way his sisters walked the world, but this... It opened bigger possibilities.

Rafe looked down at the diary. "Is this what you were afraid of with grandfather? Why you closed the Gateway? If she can move my ship along the pathways with a map, what could he have done, I wonder?" Rafe traced a finger along the leather cover, unease warring with doubt and anger. He tucked the book in his pocket, plucked his keys from a hook on the wall and left his quarters, locking the door behind him.

Three-quarters of an hour later, as the crew settled down, coping with the situation, and Rafe read the diary, the ship lurched and listed, banking right. A jolt ran through the decks and down deep into the keel. Rafe jumped to his feet from where he was sitting on the quarterdeck steps.

"To duty, men! It looks like we're coming about, and out of the conduit! Man the sail, boys, and send someone below to rouse the gunners! I want them sharp in case of trouble." He turned his head. "Look lively, Anders. No telling when we'll regain control of the ship. I want an attentive helmsman when we do."

One-Eyed Anders tilted his chin up, straightened his spine and set his feet in a wide stance on deck. He grasped the wheel in a grip that threatened to crack the wood and said, "Aye, Captain, I'll be ready."

Rafe nodded and moved his gaze back to the prow of his ship, his breath even. He tucked the diary in his pocket, his fingers trembling. Behind him he sensed Blackthorne, and together they waited.

A small glimmer of pale light shone in the darkness, growing wider as they travelled forward. The momentum of the ship slowed as the radiance grew ever nearer before exploding in a shower of illumination. Another portal appeared and the ship sailed through, suddenly airborne, flying through the sky above a strange sea. They swirled downward on black misty air currents and landed softly as if every inch of wood and metal were as light as a feather. The *Jewel* rocked on the water gently and the shimmers of magic faded into nothing.

"I have control of the helm, Captain!" came the shout from Anders, and Rafe let out the breath he had been holding. He turned and nodded.

"Keep her steady, Mr. Anders. Until we get our bearings." Rafe glanced over the lower deck. "The rest of you men tend to the sails and your duty! Until we know where we've landed, I want the ship slowed to a crawl."

The transfixed stupor that held the crew during the voyage seemed to rupture at his words and the men bustled about attending to the ship. Rafe leaned on the rail, watching, waiting. He felt the air around him crackle in some unseen impetus, a singularity about to break.

He closed his eyes for a moment, breathing in and letting his ears adjust to the noise of the ship. The familiar scent of sea and salt hit his nostrils, with a curious hint of flora that prickled at the back of his throat. The creaks and groans, grunts and banter put him more at ease, and he opened his eyes to look at the sky and feel the breeze on his face. As he stared at the clouds, a shadow soared past and a screeching cry echoed over the ship.

An answering cry came from one of the crew. "'Tis an eagle! A good omen surely."

More eyes turned upward, watching the bird's flight, as it made its way towards the *Celestial Jewel.*

"It's headed straight for us!"

And indeed, the majestic bird circled the ship before swooping in low across the deck, weaving expertly between sailors. Rafe spied something clutched in its talons, and then a scroll of paper plopped to the deck. The eagle then soared back into the sky and disappeared into the clouds.

Rafe walked down to the lower deck and plucked the message from the boards. He held a stiff roll of paper tied with a red ribbon, his name penned on the outside. He undid the ribbon and unrolled the paper, recognizing his father's handwriting. He read the scrawled words aloud.

"To unlock the map of the Lost Sea given to you by your mother, say the Lament of the Stars."

"The Lament of the Stars? What's that, sir?" Rafe looked over at Pinky Jasper's inquiring expression.

"It's an old song my father taught me." Rafe rolled up the message and stuffed it in his pocket. "And it seems to be the key to continuing our journey." He turned and nodded at Blackthorne. "I'll be below deck seeing if I can get us a map to navigate by." He turned and went below to his quarters.

He unlocked the door and gently pushed it open. The map no longer hovered in the air but sat on top of his desk as if it was any normal chart. He entered, shutting the door behind him, and settled down in his chair, staring at the sheet of paper.

"So you just magically hijack us and now you're back to being a customary, if inscrutable, map. Waiting for a key to unlock all your secrets." He ran a finger along the edge of the paper. "What will happen if I sing to you, then? Will you take us somewhere else or fly us to the stars? Or will it all turn out to be a prank, leaving us to rot in this forsaken sea?"

Rafe sighed and closed his eyes. He let his mind drift backwards, sailing into his childhood, the voice of his father crooning to him under his sister's moon. He wet his lips and sang.

> The Night has come
> in sweet refrain
> and shines the brightest moon.
> The Night has come
> in dark repose
> and flickers the shining stars.
> For in the dark,
> will the light shine clear?
> For in the dark,
> light will show the way.
> The stars will call
> against the night,
> the stars, they are the path.
> The stars will glow
> against the night,
> the stars they are your way.

Rafe opened his eyes and looked down at the map. It glowed a soft yellow light, and as he stared, the surface shifted into a more conventional chart, with landmarks and navigation markings writing themselves onto the paper, including a crude representation of the *Celestial Jewel*. Rafe leaned over the chart, studying it. He traced a finger over the marking of his ship and a map route blossomed in red from that position to an island marked *Gateway*.

"So is this where you want me to go?"

He examined the route, calculating distance and currents from the now functional map, determining the course for the ship and the bearings for Anders. Then he rolled the map in his hand and went topside to the quarterdeck.

He strode to One-Eyed Anders and handed him the map. "I believe we now have the proper navigation chart." As Anders examined the map with a shocked expression crossing his face, Rafe relayed the coordinates he worked out.

"Sounds good, Captain. Seems in order, though I never charted off something so fickle before. Hope we can trust the damn thing."

"So do I, Mr. Anders, so do I." Rafe sighed. "In any case, we haven't much choice. Lay in a course and we'll see what comes of it, shall we?"

"Aye, Captain." With another glance at the map Anders tucked the paper away in his pocket and turned the wheel of the ship, heading southeast.

Rafe turned to the crew, who still seemed at a bit of a loss for direction. "Step lively, men, and tend to your duties. Get those sails trimmed to the wind. I want speed, and plenty of it!"

At his echoing orders the crew sprang to their duties

and the familiar hum of the ship returned, with every crank, grunt, flap of sail and squeak of the rigging. Rafe blew out a slight breath and walked to stand at the rail, looking down at the lower deck.

"Where are we headed?" The expected voice of Blackthorne spoke at his shoulder as if on cue. Rafe smiled. Even in uncertainty he could count on the predictability of his first mate.

"To a hidden island and, I believe, a gateway between realms. My father is most likely waiting there."

"Well, that doesn't sound too bad. A nice sail to an island."

Rafe turned his head, a quirk of a smile on his lips. "You think so?"

"Aye. Be a quiet change of pace after sea monsters, walking corpses, and Raven Rock. Unless, of course, there are more monsters waiting to greet us. Then it will be business as usual."

Rafe gave a low chuckle, his spirits lifted. "I shouldn't think we'll find any monsters. My father certainly doesn't qualify, even as imposing and formidable as he may be."

"Then we should enjoy the sail, sir." Blackthorne inhaled deeply. "Look around. The sky's as blue as I've ever seen and the waters are calm and clear. There's a favourable wind to fill the sails and the air is balmy and smells as sweet as honey. Even if we were, um, diverted here, this is a lovely place."

Rafe glanced up at the sky and out at the seas. "What are you talking about? The sky is full of grey clouds, the wind cold, and the seas are murky."

"Sir?" Blackthorne frowned, puzzlement written on his face. "It is a beautiful day. Not a grey cloud in sight."

Rafe started, for a moment convinced his first mate had gone mad. Then he wondered if he had lost his senses before Anders spoke up.

"I'm seeing blue skies, but dark waters, sirs. I'm thinking our senses can't be trusted, perhaps?"

Rafe inhaled. "We're all seeing different surroundings?" At their nods, plus others in the crew, he let out his breath. "I reckon it's magic then, in the air itself. If I'd hazard a guess, it changes the view based on the person's mood."

Blackthorne frowned. "Why in the world would—"

"Sir!" An anxious bleat interrupted from the quarterdeck steps. Blackthorne and Rafe turned to see Elwen standing there. The man fidgeted under their gaze, wringing his hands, but blurted, "A message, sir, from Commander Pelham, guardedly inquiring as to our whereabouts and why we departed the pirate foray so abruptly. I am unable to provide an adequate explanation. I am not even certain as to where we are, let alone what happened." He paused, chewing his lip. "However, I do think we should send a hasty reply, as it appears the spellcaster message was delayed by, uh," Elwen looked around, as if finally seeing his new surroundings, before continuing without missing a step, "whatever mode of travel we employed. It is about an hour old."

"By the shoals, I forgot all about Pelham and the pirates!" Rafe sprang past Blackthorne, and dashed for the stairs, grabbing Elwen as he moved down the steps. "Come along, Elwen, we have a message to send to the Royal Navy."

<hr>

Rafe stared at the frazzled image of Pelham wavering within the spellcaster's mirror. Despite the poor clarity, Rafe was rather impressed Elwen had been able to bridge the distance from the Lost Sea through the Southern Mists. Pelham, on the other hand, was neither impressed nor in a good mood.

"The bloody pirates got away! Hit us with some damnable magic fire and bloody got away! We were lucky to have escaped without ships sunk, and as it was two were put out of commission. We scoured the seas as best we could but they're gone, vanished to who knows where. We had the bloody bastards between us. We could have crushed them! What in blazes were you thinking? What the hell happened!"

Rafe grimaced slightly, old ire rising. He squashed it down and replied, "My apologies, Commander. I know it looks as if I deserted you, but I had no hand in our disappearance. The ship was unexpectedly commandeered by other magical forces. We didn't depart of our own accord, sir, and we didn't intend to abandon the fight. Or toss this whole pirate mess in your lap, but I'm afraid that's where it landed. We are unharmed, but it's unlikely we'll be returning to help any time soon."

"What?" Rafe felt Pelham's outrage across the divide. "Why the hell not? Where are you?"

"We ended up in the Lost Sea." Rafe said the words calmly, but the shock on Pelham's face conveyed the enormity of his words.

"The Lost Sea? I—I... But that's impossible."

"Not anymore." Rafe shrugged.

"I see." Pelham sighed. "It seems you are out of this nasty mess, at least for now."

Rafe leaned forward. "How bad is it? What did Morgan do?"

Pelham straightened his shoulders. "From what we've gathered Morgan attacked Stallion Bay. My fleet is headed there now and should be arriving shortly. What little we gleaned from a woman who had been a captive of Morgan, it looks like a massacre. If her accounts are true, there won't be much to do but bury the dead. It won't be an easy thing." Pelham sighed, adding, "He may have attacked other settlements as well."

Rafe clenched his jaw. "Prepare yourself. It's doubtful Morgan would have left survivors. My sympathies, Commander. I suspect you'll have some horrific sights waiting for you."

"No doubt..." Pelham turned his head as if something distracted him and then turned his attention back. "I have to take my leave, Captain, pressing matters. Good luck with your situation."

"And good luck with yours." The spellcaster magic cut off as the last word left his mouth. Rafe pushed out of his chair and rose to his feet. He smiled at Elwen. "Thank you. I know that must have been difficult."

"Odd perhaps, but not overly hard. The magic was just...slower and stranger."

"That's good to hear, as I may need you to contact the navy again soon."

Rafe nodded to Elwen and took his leave, returning to the quarterdeck.

◆

A few hours later the *Celestial Jewel* lay in anchor in a quiet, picturesque harbour off a lush island of green forests. Looking out, Rafe now saw clear, calm waters, but darkened shadows shifted along the shore, and red-tinged clouds drifted through the sky above.

"What now, sir?" Blackthorne leaned against the rail beside him.

Before Rafe could answer, Anders interrupted. "You may want to look at the map. The damned thing's gone and changed again. 'Tis a map of the island out yonder, now. Leastwise I think it is."

Rafe turned to see Anders holding out the map. He walked over, took it, and unfurled the paper. The parchment shimmered, now revealing a topographical map of what appeared to be the island. A small marked spot to the east glowed red.

From behind his shoulder, Blackthorne asked, "Should I prepare a longboat, sir, for an inland excursion?"

Rafe shook his head. "Best I go alone." He rolled the map and handed it back to Anders, who tucked it into a pocket. "Keep the ship at anchor, unless you spot trouble. In that case, take what actions are needed and have the spellcaster send up a signal for me to return."

Blackthorne nodded, adding, "Aye, Captain."

Rafe walked to the far edge of the quarterdeck, looking out at the sea. He took a breath and shouted, "You have the ship until I return, Mr. Blackthorne." Summoning his magic, he rose into the air. He banked around the ship and headed inland.

Rafe flew over the trees, trailing blue shimmers of magic, until he found the place marked on the map. He hovered in the sky, staring down at a ragged clearing, a courtyard, and a temple. He spied movement in the shadows of a doorway and slowly lowered himself to the ground.

He landed gracefully on his feet, and to his surprise, a figure walked out to greet him. His throat grew tight, his jaw clenched and he unconsciously curled his hands into fists. Then he took a breath and spoke.

"Hello, Father."

Chapter Fourteen
Truth

"Son. I'm glad you've arrived. Not too unsettled, I hope, after the unorthodox journey?"

"Unorthodox?" Rafe snorted, sarcasm dripping off his words. "Is that what you call having my ship hijacked by Mother and its crew abducted to the end of the world?"

"What?" Reis inhaled sharply. "Damn her. I told her to convince you, not force you to come. What happened?"

"We did talk, but it ended in a disagreement." Rafe drew his lips in a thin line and glared. "I didn't like her attempt at manipulation. Or the lies you both have been feeding me over the years. I wanted truth from her, which she was unwilling to give."

Reis sighed. "And no doubt you stormed off, at which point she took matters into her own hands and sent you here unwillingly."

"Something like that, yes." Rafe shuffled his feet, glancing at the ground and then back to his father. "But I couldn't just turn my back on my duties, not with Black

Axe Morgan back."

Reis wrinkled his brow. "Who—? Oh, yes, that resurrected pirate who killed the island's latest guardian. You knew him?"

"I'm the one who killed him the first time around. Ripped his soul out of his body and cast it into the world to wander." Rafe ground his teeth slightly. "Apparently, I should have kept better track of it."

"Is that what she told you?" Reis shook his head. "No wonder you got angry. Son, that lost soul of a pirate and dozens like him have been here for years, drawn in by the necromancer. As distasteful as it was, I allowed him to practice his arts as long as he took only wayward souls and kept them contained. If anyone was lacking in duty, it was me. This necromancer took his experiments too far and allowed the pirate to get the better of him." Reis sighed again. "I found the poor man's head in a jar in the temple."

"You knew this necromancer was actively practicing his forbidden magic? Magic you banned, I might add?"

"I know, but the situation was complicated. Have you read the diary yet? Your mother was supposed to pass it along to you."

Rafe slipped a hand in his pocket, fingering the leather of the book mentioned. Since coming to the Lost Sea, he had taken to keeping it in his pocket, close to him. He pulled out the book and showed it to his father, the old feelings of resentment welling like bile in his throat.

"I read your entries. I know what you did and what you lied about." Rafe waved the journal in the space between them. "Was any of it true? The histories written by the mortals, the stories you told me as a child. Or was it all just lies woven to hide the misdeeds of my mother and grandfather, and that accursed Crow?"

Reis sighed for a third time, a quiet sound like the

tide rolling on shore. "The mortal histories, my stories, they all hold a kernel of the truth, just told from different perspectives, rewoven by years and, perhaps, wishful thinking. We all colour the truth with our own outlook. I may have painted my father with brighter hues than he deserved, but I never intended to lie." Reis lifted a hand to his son, as if offering an accord, but then dropped it to his side. "And some truths shouldn't be told to children. They must come in their own time."

"And now is the time, I suppose?" Rafe sneered.

"It is. The events started by Death, the Crow, my father and myself, have come full circle to you." Reis took a few steps forward, and this time he did raise a hand, placing it gently on his son's shoulder. "I wish you didn't have to reap the consequences, but you're the only one who can save the worlds."

Rafe backed away, bewilderment scrawled on his face. "Me? What can I do?"

Reis exhaled, a delicate sound of regret and guilt. "Much more than you realize. Much more than you remember." He moved forward, small sparks of silver snapping around his fingertips. "I'm sorry. For what I did, and for this."

In one swift movement, Reis laid a hand on the side of Rafe's head, magic penetrating into his son's mind. Reis whispered, "*Coiwych.*"

Rafe stiffened, his spine shuddering. Inside his thoughts, a long-shuttered door opened, and repressed memories flooded his mind. Images of the Crow, and his father, of seeing the Realm of the Stars and other wonders. Of wandering the pathways between worlds farther than he ever thought possible and of being within the substance of the fabric of existence, of controlling it. He wielded a power he had forgotten he possessed and did it all with ease as a mere child.

Rafe fell to his knees, his mind fully restored. "What did you do to me?" He shook, his hands trembling, his voice cracking. Memories, thoughts, feelings, knowledge of powers long concealed kept surging back in an unleashed tide. He stood in isolation, welling in hurt, regret and anger, every inch of him wanting to scream in the pain of betrayal.

"What I needed to do. To protect my child." Reis' face showed no sign of emotion. "You have every right to be angry, suppressing your memories is an unforgivable thing. But the risk of leaving them intact was too great. As a child, the full extent of your abilities put you in danger."

"I—I..." Rafe stumbled over his words. "How could you? Why?"

"To protect you from the Crow's tricks. To protect the world. Above all, you needed to be safe. Without you the realms would end."

Rafe lowered his head, his jaw clenched. His haunted voice whispered, "I don't understand."

"No. I've kept you away from all this to safeguard you, and hoping it would never come to this. A foolish hope, as we are here." Reis sighed, his shoulders bent. "It began with my father and will end by you, my son."

Rafe raised his head. "What? What is this all about?"

"Balance. Survival. Preventing the destruction of all the realms." Reis rubbed his neck. "When Ulerne came to the Realm of Eternal Night, he changed it so fundamentally, the delicate stability between the realms irrevocably altered. It has been in flux ever since. I have protected it as best I could, in part by sealing the Gateway, but a more permanent solution has always been needed. One only you can provide."

Rafe pursed his lips. "Because of—of what I can do?" He frowned, the restored memories boggling his mind. He still wasn't sure of what exactly he *could* do now. It felt as if his power was limitless.

Reis nodded. "Your ability to see the realms, feel their presence, control their currents is key."

"How? What you want... I have no idea what to do. I don't understand what I am anymore," Rafe snapped, letting some of his resentment out. A single moment and everything had changed. "Even with this new...old...this ability? And if this is such an issue why wait until now?"

"Because this isn't something you can splice together like a broken mast. All the pieces must come together precisely, in the right order and at the right time. You, the realms, your mother, and...the Crow."

"The *Crow*? You're working with him?" Rafe's voice trembled.

"Of course not." Reis scoffed. "More setting a trap. And waiting patiently. Very, very patiently. That bloody bird is such a conundrum to me, so slow in his actions. His destiny is hard to read, hard to influence, perhaps because he is at the centre of this. The best I've been able to do is steer him along the right path and wait."

"And there was no other way?" Rafe shot his father a look of disbelief. "He has to be involved?"

"He is bound in our destiny as much as we are in his."

"Ridiculous!" Rafe's anger exploded out in one word. "This sounds like more of your manipulations and lies! You bring me here against my will, reveal these things and I'm supposed to believe you? None of this makes any sense. Why are you doing this?"

"Because it needs doing."

The words struck a chord with Rafe and he scowled. "It just seems sudden. Forced even. Like a trick." Rafe rose, kicking at the ground, feeling cantankerous.

Reis' expression turned stern. "It isn't sudden at all,

or a trick. The balance shifted many centuries ago, but our worlds are slow moving. It has taken this long to come to a crisis, and for the threat to be noticed by…others." Reis lifted his chin slightly, the edges of his eyes glowing in a white sheen. "I've been holding it at bay for as long as possible, waiting for you, for the Crow, for all of us to be ready. Now is that time. I need you to join me, to become who you were meant to be."

Rafe glared at his father, a petulant sneer sliding across his mouth. "And if I refuse? Just walk away?"

"That's your choice." Reis shrugged. "But as I said, other beings are trying to shift the realms. I've been holding the line, but I've also been slowly losing the battle. This day has been coming a long time."

Reis looked directly at his son. Rafe saw the lines in his face, the sorrow in his eyes. He also saw the worry and the fear. Rafe cast his eyes to the ground, inhaled and let out the breath.

"You've been fighting this imbalance? All these years?" Rafe pushed a pebble with his boot. "And now it's my turn, is it? To fight? Why? Because of a family legacy? Atonement? How are we any part of this?" He glanced up, accusation in his eyes.

Reis only smiled. "This has nothing, and everything, to do with our family. And, my unseeing son, I am part of everything." He laughed. "Who do you think I was in the Realm of the Stars? Not Sovereign of the Gods, certainly."

"I—I never thought—" Rafe stopped talking, red creeping into his cheeks with a bit of embarrassment.

"You never even considered I had another life before, did you?"

Rafe shook his head.

"Well, I did. A life, a home and duties, just as you have here. Destiny was, and is, my charge, son. I see it all, the patchwork of the worlds, and give it a nudge here, a push there to move events the way they need to be."

Reis chuckled again at Rafe's shocked look. "My responsibilities here are no different: I shape events to their destiny. The coming of the Crow, the Shadow Bird, only made my calling more difficult."

Rafe frowned, stepping back, turning away. His breath came quickly, fighting against his tumultuous emotions. Part of him wanted to run, find a spot in the woods and think.

Instead, he glanced back and asked, "If you shape destiny, then why didn't you stop the Crow from the very beginning? Stop all this from happening? You could have, if you are what you say."

Reis shook his head. "Even I am not infallible. I did not foresee the Shadow Bird's effect on the balance of the realms. I do not know why, but my lack of sight is the reason. Perhaps he was tied too closely to my own destiny, the catalyst to bring me here to this new world."

"What do you mean?"

"Why do you think your grandfather sent me here, of all his children or followers? Because he thought this world would be *his* destiny and wanted me to shape that path for him. He meant to use me and my gifts for his own gain." Reis scowled. "I made certain he did not succeed." His shoulders slumped slightly. "My only regret is your involvement. I had hoped to spare you, alter your fate somehow, but it was never to be. That is your choice. Take up the mantle and save us, or let the realms fall."

"But-but..." Fear clutched at Rafe's gut and he shook his head. "How do I fix the realms if you cannot?"

Reis smiled. "You're the only one who can. I knew it from the moment you came into existence. The power in you—it is so different from ours. Not even Chaos or

Harmony tap into such primeval energies. That's part of why I repressed your memories. A child should not have such power."

Rafe bristled. "It was still wrong."

"Perhaps, but it shaped who you are, your integrity. I would not change that." Reis straightened his spine and tilted his chin up.

"You put too much faith in me. I am not that strong." Rafe's lip trembled and he curled his fingers.

Reis laughed. "Of course you are. What you do out there with your mortals, that magic you wield, it barely touches the extent of what you can do. You are Life and Death. Creation and Unmaking." Reis took one step closer to his son. "You have three choices. You can do nothing, let events play out as they will and live with the consequences. You can seal each realm shut. Make them separate. Lock it all away and hope the seals remain shut forever. Or you can claim your power, restore the balance, and remake worlds."

"How?"

"By using the original dark Chaos energy that caused the rift. The power of the Shadow Bird."

Rafe gasped but Reis ignored the interruption.

"Before this world existed, there were three realms of Chaos and three realms of Harmony. Because of the Shadow Bird and Ulerne, three realms of Harmony exist, but only two realms of Chaos, and whatever we are. You need to take the Crow's power, raw material if you will, and create a balancing realm of Chaos. With that source, your power will do the rest."

"Well, doesn't that sound easy." Rafe sneered.

"Hardly." Reis grinned, startling his son. "But considerably easier than the centuries of planning and manipulating I've done to bring us all into place." Reis sighed. "But my work is over, I've done all I can. You must walk the path alone from here."

Rafe frowned. "What does that mean?"

"It means reach out. Walk the realms. See what is happening for yourself. Tap into who you are and travel through all the worlds. Then make your decision."

Reis held out a hand. "Come with me and let me show you what needs to be done."

Rafe ignored his father's outstretched hand, but nodded. "Very well. Show me."

Reis lowered his arm and turned towards the temple. "Follow me."

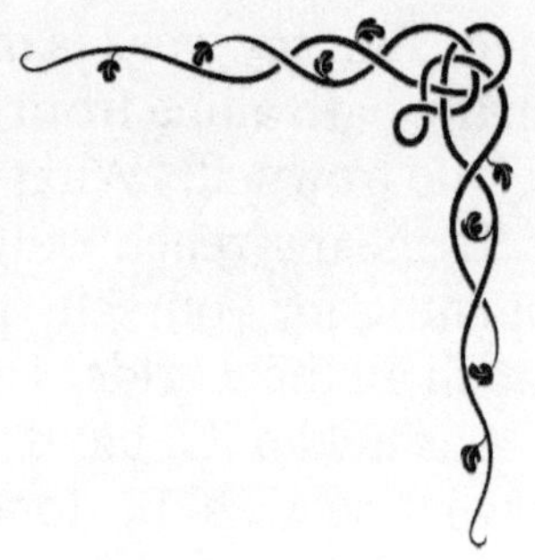

Chapter Fifteen
Pelham

From the prow of the *Star's Hope*, his jaw clenched and his fingers curled into fists, Pelham stared at the grisly trophies lining the docks of Stallion Bay. Behind him a silent crew looked on, some with their eyes forward to witness the horror, others with their heads bowed for the dead.

Pelham hissed through gritted teeth, "Bastards."

Movement in the harbour caught his attention and he saw Lynna bobbing in the water, her arms folded, her head bowed. He took one last look before turning around to face his crew.

"Prepare the longboats, men. We're going ashore to clean up this mess." He glanced to his right, and snapped, "Mr. Buckley! Signal the fleet! Put together shore parties! And make sure they have strong stomachs. There will no doubt be more carnage in the town."

Pelham's first mate snapped a salute and barked immediate orders. Squeals and clanks of the winches sounded and the flagman signalled the other navy ships, advising them of Pelham's orders.

"Buckley!" At Pelham's call the lanky, angular man rushed to his captain's side.

"Sir? Orders, sir?" The first mate straightened his spine and squared his shoulders, eager to please.

"Did the spellcaster get the word out? Have the islands been alerted?"

"Aye, sir. I checked on that the moment we reached harbour, sir. Warnings went out to the Outlaw Keys, the Wakeford Islands, and the Outer Islands. All navy ships are on high alert for the pirates. And advised of the—the magic, sir. That we are dealing with dangerous magic."

"Good work, Buckley." Pelham nodded his approval and for a brief second his first mate smiled. "How's the woman that was rescued?"

Buckley frowned. "Traumatised. She's down below in a berth. Ship's doctor gave her a sleeping draught. For the best, I think, considering. No need for her to relive the horror."

"Quite right. Bad enough we'll need to do it." Pelham sighed, adding, "As soon as the boats are ready I'll lead the shore parties. You'll have the ship."

Buckley's chest rose as he inhaled. In the exhalation he replied with a smart, "Yes, sir!"

Pelham walked away across the deck to watch the longboats swing into position and the organization of the crew going ashore. His mind seethed in anger and outrage and he muttered softly, "We'll get these bastard pirates. The navy will hunt them down and send every misbegotten ship to the bottom of the sea."

❖

The navy longboats rowed into Stallion Bay and landed on nearby beaches or tied up by the few intact docks. As they moved across the docks, the sailors stayed silent; not a word, a jest, or expletive. As if the ruthless horror of what they saw stole their voices, or their anger choked off their words. Only Pelham spoke, and only to give orders.

"Gather the heads. Wrap them in cloth and find a place to store the remains. The harbourmaster building looks like it's still standing." He gestured to a damaged but durable building farther along the wharf. "See if that will do to give the dead some respect."

"Aye, Captain," came the replies, and Pelham glanced out at the harbour. Lynna was still there, treading water. He didn't blame her for not coming ashore. This was a sight no one should witness. He watched her for a moment or two before shouts and the sound of retching yanked his attention back to the situation at hand.

He saw his men staring at the harbourmaster's and two sailors doubled over gagging. He rushed over, shouting, "What's happened? What's wrong?"

One man choked out, "Inside, sir, inside." He pointed with a shaky finger before he turned his head away.

Pelham took a breath to steady his nerves and stepped within the building. The smell hit him first. The sharp copper stench of blood mixed with human guts and the beginning of rot. He stopped almost immediately, his face blanching, his stomach queasy, the bile rising into the back of his throat. He wanted to shut his eyes against the appalling sight, but he forced himself to look. Forced himself to witness the dead, mutilated remains of the harbourmaster.

The poor woman's severed head sat on her desk, her eyes gouged out, her tongueless mouth wedged open with a small peg. The removed parts, eyeballs and tongue, were lined up beside the head, sitting on a ship's manifest. The woman's torso sat in her chair behind the desk and her severed legs stuck out from beneath. Her arms hung from the ceiling, suspended from hooks and streaked with dried blood. Beneath her discoloured limbs were dried stains of more blood.

Anger welled inside him, more fury than he had ever felt in his life. He yelled, "Get me a cloth to cover this poor wretch," and grabbed a nearby chair. He pulled out his knife, yanked the chair over to the desk and climbed on top of it. He cut down the woman's limbs and laid them tenderly beside the rest of her. By then a sailor had brought a large swath of sailcloth and Pelham draped it gently over the entire desk.

"Atrocities. The lot of this. The bastards committed atrocities. Hanging or sinking is too good for them. They should be staked out in the Stone Fire Islands and left to burn." He shook his head and walked outside for fresh air. Among his men once more, he gave an order. "Bring the other remains here, to lay with the poor harbourmaster. We need to see about any survivors. We'll sort out the dead for proper burial later."

He looked towards the harbour and noticed Lynna was missing. A small hint of sadness and disappointment tingled at the back of his mind until he noticed a commotion in the water by one of the docks. Then Lynna's voice shouted his name.

"Augustus! I found another body in the harbour!" She hauled the corpse of a man into the shallows. This one also had missing appendages and had been well nibbled by the fishes.

Fury again sparked in Pelham and he snapped at a pair of sailors close at hand. "You two, go help her get the body ashore. And then lay it to rest with the others!" Then he barked at another group of sailors, "You lot come with me! We will head into town and see what other horrors these damnable pirate bastards left us!" He strode past the startled sailors, who scrambled to catch up. "By the gods, I'll hunt these scum to the end of the worlds and see them pay for this!"

Pelham stood on a Stallion Bay dock, looking out to sea. Below, in the harbour, Lynna swam in gentle circles. Behind them both, in the silhouette of the setting sun, his sailors helped the surviving townsfolk prepare the dead for burial. Agonized sobs and strident wails sometimes broke the silence.

Pelham cleared his throat, more to stopper his emotions than anything. "Do you know what they are doing back there, Lynna?"

The Goddess of the Sea stopped swimming and looked up at the naval officer. She replied with one word, "No."

"They are matching heads to bodies so people can bury their dead. Some remains are simply being prepared for decent internment, unmourned, because no one is left. Whole families! Those butchers murdered whole families. Women, men, children. Brutally and for no reason other than to kill."

Lynna sighed, a soft sound that echoed as deep as the ocean. "How many survived?"

"Our last count was forty-seven. From a town of close to two hundred people." Pelham shook his head, his voice harsh. "How did they massacre so many? Even at five ships full to capacity, the townspeople should have been able to fight back against the pirates."

Lynna splashed at the water. "Perhaps not. A surprise attack, peppered with cannon fire. And at night, by my reckoning. They would have been shocked, most even asleep. Armed men suddenly upon them. It's not hard to imagine people trying to run instead of fight, or being caught unawares with no defence." She paddled through the water, drawing a bit closer to the dock. "Not every soul is trained to respond well to an attack. Or has the skill to fight back."

"That's true." Pelham's tone softened. "They may have thought more about hiding, about protecting their families. Not that it did them a bit of good." He looked back to see a young man weeping openly over a severed head of an elderly woman. "Look at them. The ones that still live. How do you move on from such a thing? Perhaps the dead are the lucky ones."

"If they moved on to the After World. But there are ghosts out there, Augustus. I can see flitting shades wandering through town. I haven't dared look too close, lest my heart breaks any further."

Pelham gasped slightly. "I hadn't thought of that. Damnation." He paused, his brow furrowed. "There isn't a temple here in town, but I believe there is one on the island. When I return to the ship, I'll see the spellcaster and make arrangements to have temple priests come here." He gave a quick glance over his shoulder at the sound of more weeping. "It may be helpful for the survivors as well."

"Thank you."

"It is the least we can do, perhaps the only thing left to do. I never thought I'd say this, but I wish your brother was here. He's better at dealing with settlements than I am. Give me a sailor, a ship or a crisis and I know what to do. Give me the aftermath of a tragedy and the grieving and I'm at a loss." Pelham crossed his arms and stared out to sea.

Lynna splashed at the water. "They'll take comfort in the navy's presence. It will ease their fear. And you're better at this than you give yourself credit for, better than me." She sighed. "Although I wish Rafe was here as well.

He is better at this than we are."

"I fear he has his hands full, dealing with whatever pulled him away."

"His mother. I recognized the trace of her magic lingering in the ocean." Pelham glanced down, a quizzical look on his face, hearing the fear in her voice. She shook her head. "Best you stay far away from it. My stepmother is not someone you ever wish to meet."

Pelham shrugged, but only replied, "You have a very odd family."

Lynna smiled slightly. "I know."

Chapter Sixteen
The Realms

Reis walked to the side of the temple and pressed his hand against a rune, his fingers glowing in silver light. The stone appeared to melt into a glow and transformed into a shimmering doorway leading...somewhere.

Reis looked at his son. "I created this chamber to follow the threads of fate intertwining the realms. Come and see?"

Glaring, Rafe grudgingly said, "I suppose."

Reis nodded at Rafe and disappeared through the doorway.

Rafe hesitated for a split second before striding after his father. As he passed through to the other side, the magic behind him faded and vanished, leaving him standing with his father in a dimly lit room.

Rafe looked around, barely making out walls and a few shapes in the poor lighting. "What is this place?"

"This is a scrying room, where I've been observing the realms for a very long time. I built this with the first guardian."

"A scrying room?" Rafe was curious despite his anger.

Reis smiled and snapped his fingers. The room illuminated in an otherworldly light, revealing a huge hexagonal-shaped space. Patterns and runes decorated the walls and floor and the three columns evenly spaced around the room.

"This is a space between realms, a tiny corner I carved out to study and interact with the realms without being noticed. Here I can open a window into each realm. Watch."

Reis conjured a sphere of silver energy and tossed it at one of the columns. The pillar flashed in sudden illumination, and images danced along its surface and along the wall behind it.

"There it is, my former home. The Realm of the Stars." Reis smiled wistfully.

Rafe stared at the images dancing along the chamber wall in shining pale shades. They glittered and shimmered, reflecting glorious stars and burnished radiance. Each scene glowed from perfect beauty that captured his heart. In that instant he understood the Crow's obsession.

Then the images faded and for a moment he felt hollow. His father's voice broke the spell.

"Here is where I kept watch and altered destiny when I could, but now the true purpose of this place can happen. This is where you will realign the worlds."

"Just like that?" Rafe's shoulders stiffened and his voice rose in pitch slightly. "What do I do, then? Wave my hand and make it better?" His voice cracked in bitterness. "I'm not sure I even believe any of this."

"Then perhaps you should see for yourself." Reis retorted, a mildly disapproving tone to his voice. "Test your power inside the chamber, see where it takes you. For you, this place will be a gateway to travel where you will.

Walk the realms. See what is happening for yourself. Then make your decision."

Reis waved his hand and a portal shimmered into view, crackling the air. He stepped through it and was gone. Rafe stood in the chamber alone, gaping at the now empty space.

His first instinct was to leave, rebel against his father, his mother, and all his obligations. But he didn't. He ground his teeth in frustration and exhaled.

"I never asked for this!" His shout echoed off the walls. "Any of this! Not duty! Not destiny! Not saving the realms! What kind of parents force this responsibility on their child? What kind of fate is that?"

Then Rafe hung his head and whispered, "Mine. My fate."

He stared at the floor, white marble streaked with blue. He raised a hand, snapping similarly coloured blue sparks off his fingertips into the air. They danced for a moment, suspended, before falling and hitting the stone. Reflections of realms echoed back where they contacted the floor.

Rafe sucked in a breath, and then exhaled, excitement tingling in his thoughts, despite everything. He closed his eyes, summoned his magic and sent sparks of power flying around the chamber. The room lit up in a blue glow and a thousand times a thousand images decorated the walls, opening Rafe's mind and magic to the unbounded space of Harmony and Chaos.

His essence—magic, soul and mind—floated free within the channels of energy that laced the realms together. He felt the power meld with his and he let himself fall into the nexus. He raced through the stream, awash in the primal intensity, his magic connected with the source of all divine force, the heart of both Harmony and Chaos. He inhaled a breath with both his body—still on the island—and with his quintessence that sailed infinity. With the exhale, the power he travelled shimmered, lines of darkness and light spreading like spiderwebs, showing the paths to strange nooks and crannies and the realms of the gods. Rafe reached out with nothing but a thought, an unformed question, and everything laid itself bare.

In an instant he saw, heard and felt each world encompassed in existence. The blistering heat of the Realm of Undying Flame, the cacophonic discord of the Realm of Everlasting Screams, the boundless joy in the Realm of Unending Bliss and the silence and calm of the Realm of Infinite Peace. And finally he beheld again the Realm of the Stars.

The sheer beauty of the domain stirred deep emotions, brought tears to eyes an eternity away on an island. The expanse of it glittered in iridescence, and he smelled a sweet floral fragrance mixed with a sharp tang. It glowed a soft white and silver with amber tinges and streaks, as if the moon and sun danced together. Rafe drew his focus closer, bringing himself deeper into the realm, savouring the grace and splendour of the world. He drifted, lost in the shiny sweetness until...

A note of discontent, of discord, shattered the perfection.

It started as a tingle in his magic and on his skin. His body shivered and every thought gravitated to the source: a patch of shadow at the edge of the Realm of the Stars. He extended his energy, his senses, and suddenly drew back, shocked.

Words slipped out from his disembodied voice, "The Gateway."

Somehow he knew, perceived the entrance between his world and the Realm of the Stars, sealed and cold, but there, writhing in a taint, laced in hate and anger, greed and jealousy. He pushed at it with his magic and abruptly something pushed back, revealed a hidden secret.

Lines snaked out from the poison, one weaving through the world of Light and one back down into his realm. Rafe let his mind trace the thread running through the starlight, through strange cities and magnificent cosmic wonders until he found himself staring at a gilded throne and a lone slumped figure. The man looked up as if he sensed something and Rafe saw parts of himself and his father reflected from the face.

"Ulerne." Rafe whispered the name and the man frowned.

"Is someone there?" His grandfather's voice came at him angry and hoarse. Rafe retreated without answering, back to the Gateway.

He then traced the other strand of darkness, down into his world, coming back to the seas around the Outlaw Keys. He followed the twisting wisps to five ships and a crow sitting atop a mast. The bird turned and looked at him.

The creature hissed, "God of Souls!"

The shock of the recognition snapped the connection and Rafe felt himself yanked backwards, dragged through the energy pathways and thrust back into his body. He fell to his knees, his hands on the floor of the chamber, the walls of his father's creation surrounding him, now reflecting only cold stone. A chill ran over his skin and fear churned in his gut.

"Damn him. Damn them all." The angry words slipped out as the realization sunk in. His father had told him the truth. The fabric of the realms was in turmoil. Perhaps even more so than his father knew or cared to share.

Light reflected in the corner of his eye and a shimmer caught his attention. A doorway opened and Reis walked through. "You're done then? Gone and come back? Have you made your decision?"

Rafe stood, facing his father. "I have, but I need you to tell me one thing first. Did you know about the dark threads? The ones connecting Grandfather, the Crow, and the Gateway?"

"What?" Shock shattered out with Reis' voice. "I knew there had been contamination, corruption of the pure light, but it runs that deep? To still be connected... No wonder the realms have deteriorated. Are you certain there is a vein of darkness in the Realm of the Stars?"

Rafe nodded, relief washing over him that his father had not lied about this at least.

"Then the situation is far worse than I feared. Far worse. Something of the Shadow Birds must have been left behind, a remnant from when they originally opened the Gateway. There is no turning back now. The Crow must be defeated and drained of his power, and this remnant of his removed from the Realm of the Stars." Reis stared, worry etched in his expression. "Will you do it?"

Rafe took a breath and let it out slowly. "I will."

Chapter Seventeen
Gathering Threads

Rafe brooded in his quarters, pondering everything he had learned. Above him on deck, he heard the crew's laughter and happy voices as they took in the sun and sea air with some well-earned relaxation and rum.

The leather-bound journal lay on his desk, his hand resting on the cover. He drew a thumb over the surface, feeling the texture. His father's words, spoken before he returned to the *Jewel,* echoed in his mind.

"Read the last entry I wrote for you. You'll understand better what happened and what you have to do. How you proceed from there is up to you."

Curiosity itched at his thoughts, but he hesitated to open the book. He knew once read, his course was set irrevocably and could not be altered. Rafe flexed his fingers, tapping the cover.

"What am I worried about? Responsibility? I face that every day. Failure? I know the possibility well."

"Perhaps you fear the one thing you tend to avoid."

Blackthorne's voice startled Rafe and he jerked his head up. He hadn't even heard the door open or the man enter the room. "When did you get here?"

The first mate looked sheepish. "Just arrived, sir. In time to catch your musings. I didn't mean to speak out of turn."

"You didn't, and I wouldn't mind if you elaborated further. You seem to have a better insight than I do."

Blackthorne hesitated, shoulders shifting, straightening, hands moving behind his back as if coming to attention. "Well, sir, I've been sailing with you a long time, and while I couldn't ask for a better captain, that is how you define yourself. As captain. Yet, undeniably, you are more than that and you avoid that issue when possible. From what you told me of what's required, perhaps your hesitation stems from your needing to embrace and accept your true role as a god."

Rafe stared, echoes of his own insecurities agreeing with Blackthorne's words. He didn't want to take his ordained place in whatever destiny had planned. "Perhaps you're right. I don't want to be a god. I like this life. I don't want to be something else."

"Begging your pardon, sir, why does one mean the end of the other?" Blackthorne grinned. "I mean, you're a bloody god. Seems to me you can do as you like and who's to gainsay you. For once, sir, do your duty the way you see fit, not through the eyes or actions of others. Be the God of Souls *and* the bloody captain of the *Celestial Jewel*."

Rafe stared again, this time with his mouth open. "I, um..."

"Never quite thought of it like that, did you, sir?"

Rafe shook his head.

"Might want to start." Blackthorne relaxed and nodded. "I'll take my leave now. Just came down to see how you were faring. Some of the crew were asking about you." Blackthorne turned and then stopped, looking back at Rafe. "Almost forgot. Elwen has been updating Pelham on our status and getting reports back about the pirates. They're lying low, it appears. Navy hasn't found a sign of them yet."

"Damn. Another thing to worry about. Wish I'd gotten a better glimpse of their location when I encountered the Crow." Rafe sighed. "But have Elwen keep in regular contact. As soon as I'm done figuring out what I'm to do, I'll see if Father has any thoughts on stopping our pirate friends."

"Very well, sir." With a nod, Blackthorne left Rafe's quarters, closing the door behind him.

As the door clicked shut and he was alone, Rafe sighed. Blackthorne's words about his fears twirled around in his brain. His fingers twitched and he glared at the book under his hand. "Damnation, he's right! I am a god. What am I so afraid of?" He snapped open the journal, thumbing to the pages his father told him to read.

Burdens and the legacy of consequences are all I have to offer my son. I wanted to spare him, I wanted to carry the weight of this calamity. In my hubris, I thought I would be the one to fix the imbalance, shift destiny here or there and grant the realms their returned equilibrium.

Such fallacy. The God of Destiny is nothing but a fool. I haven't the power, not even taking what I need from the Shadow Bird. Not even if I took the power of Death herself. I cannot unmake and reshape worlds. That is what needs to be done.

Yet, I will continue to fight.

For while I may not be the one, fate has seen fit to cast that mantle on my son. The visions came to me today, the day he was born. As clear as stars on a cloudless night, his role in this matter revealed itself. For all that I may wish it otherwise. On a day I should rejoice and celebrate, I feel a deep melancholy. For all I must do, for all he must experience and for all I will sacrifice. He will inherit this madness.

My poor son. Such a darling baby and so oblivious to the destiny I and others are shaping for him. I look at him with such sadness and wish I had any other choice to offer him. I could find none. So many times today I wondered if I should let the realms fall to save him the responsibility and choices he must make. The choices I must make and the distance I will put between us. I hope I can be strong enough, for him and our worlds.

So, I write this for you, my son, as a way of an explanation I can never give you as you grow, and to ask for your forgiveness.

Rafe sucked in a breath, his hands trembling. Emotions welled, his thoughts and feelings a maelstrom tempest. He stuffed his reactions in a box and kept reading.

This all began with your grandfather, Ulerne, and a creature called Dream Walker, a Shadow Bird. This being came to the Realm of the Stars with his brothers, and Ulerne welcomed the trio. We all did, fascinated by such dark creatures. We did not realize the harm their very presence created. We gave no thought to Chaos existing in a realm of Harmony, only to helping the Shadow Birds embrace the Light. We did not see how their darkness corrupted us. Not until it was too late.

By then Ulerne had succumbed. He did not go to the Realm of Eternal Night to save it. He went to conquer it, but for all, he pretended otherwise. He only failed because he was too weakened from his fight with Ashteus. He could not confront Death and win. Only then did he feign the role of saviour. He even imprisoned the monster instead of killing it in hopes of using it against Death later. He told me all his plans when he returned to the Realm of the Stars.

That is when I knew how I failed. What I failed to discern. And why I came to this new world born of Chaos and Harmony equally. I came to stop my father from destroying what he helped create. Here I found the truth of everything.

Here in this strange place that should never have existed, this world of mortals that styled itself the Seven Kingdoms and the Outer Islands, I discovered the broken pieces.

Rafe closed his eyes for a moment, breathing in and out, listening to the rhythm of the sea against his ship. He calmed his thoughts and continued.

There was Chaos, there was Harmony. All-powerful Gods who spawned three children each and granted them realms within their dominion. Six worlds: the Realm of Unending Bliss, the Realm of Infinite Peace, the Realm of the Stars, the Realm of Undying Flame, the Realm of Everlasting Screams, and the Realm of Eternal Night. Three realms against three realms, mirroring each other, creating a balance that spun our existence in perfect unison.

The system worked—for so long. Until the balance shifted when Ulerne remade the Realm of Eternal Night. This upheaval tipped the equilibrium, and the worlds tore at the edges of each other, spinning wild magic against a hair's breadth of oblivion.

That alone should have destroyed what existed, and nearly did, save for Death and myself repairing what we could and shoring up the rest. But with each century it worsens, pieces of realms colliding, interacting. I hold the tide where I can, but eventually, we will all fall.

Unless you save us, my son.

That is the destiny I saw for you when you were born. The moment you took your first breath, I saw who you were. The god to remake worlds. I named you God of Souls, but that was a lie. You are much more than that. You are the God of Creation and Unmaking. You are the one to bridge the gap, to reshape the cracks and fissures of our realms into something new, something that will include us all, Chaos, Harmony and Mortal.

Rafe closed the book and his eyes, blinking back tears. Whatever he chose to do, however he repaired the damage, he knew now this was his path and he would create the world he wanted.

***

"Something wrong, birdie?" Morgan looked up at the creature perched in the ship's rigging. "You're quiet."

"No." The Crow's raspy voice sounded anxious. "I don't know."

Morgan shrugged. "I know something spooked ya. Saw it earlier."

"It's probably nothing, just..." The Crow ruffled his feathers. "Something feels different. Altered. That worries me." He spread his wings. "I need to think, to see for myself." The Crow took flight leaving Morgan to stare after him.

He soared into the night sky, far away from pirates and the sea, edging his way from the mortal sky and shifting into the darkness between realms. There he searched for a sign of the *Celestial Jewel* and her captain, Rafe's face haunting his memories.

"How did you walk between realms so soon?" The Crow mumbled to himself as he flew. "Did she help you? Are you both working against me? Where are you?"

The Crow explored the reaches of the in-between, through cracks and crevices and insubstantial thought, peeking past dreams and worlds with no trace of his quarry, save the touch of magic he felt earlier.

He settled down into the blackness to think.

"You were there and then you weren't. And yet you found me, if only for a moment. How?" The bird flicked a wing at the shadows. "It started with her. Death." The Crow spat the word and shivered. "Yes, it started with her."

The Crow raised his head and shouted. "Stole your son away, did you? Hiding him from me? I'm flattered." He stretched his wings and hissed. "It won't work! Do you hear me? It won't work. He's out there and I will find him!"

He hissed again and suddenly shivered.

"You haven't changed." A voice floated out of mist and shadow, and Death showed herself to the Crow. "Not in all these long centuries. Still arrogant. I used to find that attractive."

The bird held his ground, despite the shaking of his wings. "Where is he? Where did you hide him?" He ruffled his feathers. "I'll find him! No matter what you've done!"

"He's not hidden." Death smiled. "Only where he needs to be. And I know you'll find him. But not now. When the time is right." Her shadows shifted and the Crow backed away a step.

"What does that mean? What are you scheming?"

"No schemes. Only destiny. His and yours. The way it is meant to be."

"Bah." The Crow spat. "Destiny is for fools. I made my

own and will make it again. Not you, your son or anyone else will stop that."

Death tilted her head. "We'll see." She laughed and the temperature dropped several degrees. The Crow fluffed out his feathers. "But whatever the outcome, I have faith you'll find my son. Eventually. Even gods need their sleep, right little bird?" She laughed again and disappeared in a haze of dark mist.

The Crow smiled. "So true. And even gods dream. Thank you for the help." The Crow soared upward and flew back to the mortal world.

Chapter Eighteen
Headed North

"Blasted damnable navy!" Morgan growled and paced the quarterdeck of the *Shadow Raider*. Around him, his fellow pirates remained silent, too afraid of his aggressive and volatile mood to speak. "Made us turn tail and run like curs. Now we're hiding in this wretched little cove instead of spreading mayhem." He stared out over the rail at the small unnamed bay of Cataclysm Reef where his five ships lay anchored. "Now they're out in force looking for us, the bastards!"

"Yes, that is unfortunate." A deep raspy voice sounded from above as the Crow flew down and settled on the ship's rail. "But not an impossible setback."

Morgan scowled. "Where in all the bloody shoals have you been?" Morgan spat on the deck. "Thought you might've deserted. You took off in a blasted hurry. Like your tail was on fire."

"I had things to do." The Crow flicked a wing.

"Why'd ya come back? To gloat?"

The Crow chuckled. "No. I haven't given up on you yet, Captain. In fact, I was trying to locate our mutual friend, Captain Morrow. I sensed him for a moment and then... he disappeared." The Crow tilted his head, amused at Morgan's deepening scowl.

The pirate snarled, "What do ya mean, he disappeared? A bloody ship can't just disappear! The coward turned tail and ran, he did, and just when I had him. I need him found so I can shove my sword through his guts!"

The Crow pulled his wings against his body. "He didn't run. I believe outside forces forced his departure. But do calm yourself, I can find him and bring him to us. She can't protect him forever."

"She? There's a bloody woman involved? Some sort of witch? Not one of his bloody family?"

"No one you want to tangle with, Mr. Morgan. Best not be noticed by her if you value your hide. Leave those dealings to me. I have one last trick in my feathers, never fear."

Morgan grunted his displeasure but didn't argue. "All I want is Rafe Morrow's bleeding corpse at my feet. I don't care how it's done." He glared at the Crow. "Can you give me that, birdie?"

The Crow shifted his feet. "I believe I can. It may be trickier than we anticipated, but I can lure him out of hiding."

For a brief moment, Morgan's eyes lit up and a smile brightened his face, then his expression changed back to a miserable scowl. "Fat lot of good that will do us. We ain't nowhere near strong enough to take on him, his sister and the navy."

The Crow stretched his wings, swaying a bit in the sea breeze. "True. So we need to separate him away from his allies. Make him come to us in all haste, without ship or navy. His sister we may have to contend with."

"Got an idea, have you? My fleet against two gods?"

"Something like that." The Crow gave a soft caw.

Morgan chuckled and stepped in closer until mere inches separated man and bird. "You sure the two of us can take down Morrow?"

The Crow shifted on his perch. "Reasonably. Nothing is certain, but we are a match for him. Together."

Morgan put a hand on the rail and leaned in closer. He whispered, "Then we use the other ships and the rest of those fool pirates to attack the Sea Goddess if she comes. Divide and conquer the gods while we end that bastard Captain Morrow."

The Crow blinked and replied in an equally low voice. "Your men and ships will mostly be destroyed. You're willing to sacrifice them?"

Morgan smiled. "Aye. If it gets me what I want." He straightened and took a step back, still grinning.

The Crow gave a short laugh. "Your devious nature and treachery knows no bounds."

"Thank you, birdie. A fine compliment." Morgan eased beside the Crow, leaning against the rail. "So what's yer plan?"

"We head north. Between our two magiks we should be able to provide enough cover to evade the navy ships, I believe."

"North? Back to the Outer Islands?" The Crow nodded, and then Morgan asked, "Which one?"

"Rock Island. *His* stronghold. There is a small settlement on the southernmost tip we can attack to lure him home. If it seems like we are threatening his temple, his Oracle, he'll come. He'll not want his seer in danger. Not after what happened with the last one."

"Oh, now I like that." Morgan rubbed his chin, stroking

a few days of beard stubble. "Twist the knife before we cut out his heart." A low rumbling chortle rattled from his throat. "Too bad it can't be the Oracle." Morgan eyed the Crow. "Sure we can't take out the temple?"

"As delightful as that would be, there's a garrison of trained fighters stationed in Blue Bay, and armed guards at the temple. Taking it would not be simple. Not like an undefended settlement."

"Garrison? Guards? When did this happen?" Morgan burbled out his bewilderment. "Wait. You said something happened to the last Oracle. What?"

"The temple was invaded by armed sailors and she was murdered. In front of Captain Morrow. He took precautions after that to ensure the next Oracle's safety."

"Oh my!" Morgan clapped his hands in delight. "I wish I could have seen that. I hope she suffered."

"I'm not sure you would have enjoyed it as much as you think." The Crow's voice tinged with dark amusement. "The good captain tore out the soul from her murderer. I believe you are acquainted with that particular power of his."

Morgan blanched, the colour draining from his face and leaving his skin as pale as moonlight. His hands trembled and he gagged. He clenched his jaw and hissed. "Never speak of that! 'Tis an awful thing. You have no idea. The pain, the wretched... Just never speak of it."

The Crow gave a caw, but did not reply. He only waited until Morgan composed himself, hiding his delight in the pirate's obvious distress. He subtly watched the pirate quiver with fear and relished the shudders sliding through the man's body.

Finally Morgan stopped shaking and said, "Once we set the trap, then what? How'll he know what we did? Navy will probably get word first."

The Crow puffed out his feathers. "You leave that to me. I'll see he finds out well before the word trickles down to anyone else."

"Right then." Morgan pushed himself off the rail. "That's the plan. We head north. I'll tell the helmsman and you figure out what we're going to do to hide from the navy." He nodded at the Crow, turned on his heel and strode across the deck.

"This is a good plan, birdie. A little magic mist to help us skulk north. The navy ain't going to spot us now."

"Hopefully." The Crow said nothing else. He hadn't told Morgan about the presence he felt. Someone had been watching them as they left. At least now they were safe from prying eyes.

"Don't you worry none. We'll have smooth sailing from here."

Morgan's words proved true, for in a haze of conjured fog and spells of concealment, the pirate fleet slipped past the navy and made it to more northerly waters undetected. The midday sun beat down on the five ships and the wind blew them at full sail. When they came in sight of Rock Island, they headed past the small settlement of Shell River.

"Are you sure about this, Captain?" The hesitant voice of Finn spoke up. He stood beside Morgan on the quarterdeck. "We could just blast them with the cannon like at Stallion Bay."

"Aye, we could. And be down ammunition when the real threat shows up. Remember we'll be taking on gods, lad. We need that cannon shot for later. This way will take longer, but it'll get the job done. Besides," Morgan grinned as he finished, "the attack will be up close and personal, and more bloody. I know you like that."

Finn matched the grin. "Aye, bloody is the way I like it. Just anxious to get started at the butchering I suppose."

"Good lad." Morgan clapped his shoulder. "I like a man champing at the bit to kill." He glanced over and shouted at the helmsman, "Just out of sight of Shell River now. Then ease her in towards shore so we can heave anchor. Finn here wants those longboats headed in as soon as possible."

The helmsman grunted and kept steady on the course as did the other ships. Soon, the vessels anchored in a cove beyond Shell River and the longboats, filled with pirates, shoved off towards shore. A minimal crew remained behind to tend the ships.

Black Axe Morgan sat in the lead boat as his men grumbled and rowed, manoeuvring through the shallows and to their landing spot. The Crow flew ahead and waited for them to arrive, perched in a tree clear of the beach.

The invasion of boats hit the beach soon after, a soft rasp of wood scraping along sand with the grunts and footfalls of men hauling boats above the tide mark and into the underbrush. When the boats were stowed, Morgan signalled his men to fall in line for the march inland.

He gave the orders in a low voice, but one that carried. "Stay in tight, no stragglers. We'll follow the beach back around to the island tip, then head along the trails to the rear of the village. Birdie here says they lead right to Shell River."

He glanced up at the Crow, his expression a mix of suspicion and asking for confirmation. The Crow nodded, and Morgan turned back to his pirates. "Once we arrive, we attack. No quarter. Kill them all." He grinned at his men, the smile dark and menacing. "Every last one. I want a slaughter. No one escapes. No survivors this time."

Nods, salutes and soft whispers of, "Aye," answered him. Morgan turned around, satisfied, and headed out, leading his raiding party towards Shell River.

A long trek later, with peevish, restless men now at his back, Morgan finally espied the settlement. He let out a sigh, relief chasing away frustration. "There she is, boys, Shell River." Murmurs rippled among his pirates and Morgan felt the wave of excitement and anticipation grow. "Weapons ready, now. When we hit the crest of that ridge ahead, we will scope out the lay of the land, then charge in, swords swinging."

The company of men crept to the ridge, bodies slouched, alert for trouble or townsfolk. Only the rodents and birds greeted them, fleeing from their presence. Even the wind stilled as they crouched on the hill, surveying the village. Finn pushed his way forward and crawled in beside Morgan, whispering, "What's the plan, sir?"

"See those outlying homesteads?" Finn nodded. "We'll hit them first. Easy pickings. Then down the main road through the square and the marketplace, fanning out to all the houses. With no spellcaster about, shouldn't be hard to keep it contained to the village."

Morgan nodded, to himself more than Finn. "We'll hit the harbour last." Morgan gestured to the small cluster of buildings and docks at the far end of the hamlet. "There ain't no cargo ships berthed, and the fishing boats are gone too. Means a lot of the village folk are out at sea." He stared up at the sky and the position of the sun. "We got an hour or two before they start coming back from the day's fishing, I reckon. Plenty of time to kill their friends and families before they return."

Finn gave a low chuckle. "And when they do come home, we'll be waiting. To add their blood to our swords."

"Aye, lad. That's the idea. Spread the word to the men and we'll get to slaughtering." Finn scurried back, winding among the men, whispering the plan as he moved. Morgan waited until everyone was ready and gave the signal to attack.

The pirates rushed down the hill, no yells or raiding cries, spreading out to all the outlying farms and cottages. They cut down people working outside and kicked in doors, murdering all occupants: mainly women, youths and children. Some pocketed small valuables, but most simply left behind corpses knowing they could return at their leisure for the spoils.

They repeated the pattern with the main village, rampaging through the streets, assaulting, killing, invading homes and butchering the innocent. They left no one alive, splattering walls, cobblestones and wood in a ghastly shade of red. They accomplished their grisly work quickly, the village ill-equipped to defend against armed pirates, ending their murderous spree on the docks. With one last villager their prisoner.

Amid gore and dead bodies Morgan and his men stood grinning over the last poor soul left alive. The harbourmaster of Shell River. The older man crouched by Morgan's feet, a ring of other pirates surrounding him. Spatters of blood stained his clothes and his greying hair. He shivered, a hand raised defensively, but did not beg for his life. Morgan put the tip of his sword under the man's chin and lifted his head.

"We killed them all, you know. Every last man, woman and child in this sorry village. Except for you. Know why?"

The harbourmaster didn't move or answer.

Morgan continued talking. "Because I need something from you before you die. I need to know how many boats and men are out there on the waters fishing. How many can we expect back for the butchery?"

Morgan shoved the blade tip harder against the man's

throat, drawing blood.

"Tell me now and I'll run this blade through your throat clean and quick. An easy death for you. Refuse and I'll torture you until you scream the information and beg me to kill you. Your choice. Either way I win. And don't think you can be brave and save them, those out fishing. Even if you somehow don't talk in time, they're still dying. It'll just take longer and be bloodier." Morgan chuckled. "But I'm feeling generous today. Make your death and theirs easy. Tell me what I want to know."

The trembling man closed his eyes. He lurched forward, straight onto Morgan's sword. The sharp blade sliced into his throat and he died in moments, gurgling and spitting blood.

"Damnation!" Morgan screamed in rage and pulled his weapon from the man's flesh. He hacked at the body repeatedly, cutting great slices into the corpse, mutilating the remains and splashing his men in warm blood.

Then he looked up, wild green fire in his eyes and blood streaks on his face. "Search his office, see if you can find anything on the fishing boats! And get this place ready for an ambush! The minute these villagers get home they're going to die! And I want it brutal!"

His men jumped to obey, and Morgan stepped over the remains of the harbourmaster, giving the body a kick as he did. He glared out at the sea. "Yeah, I want it brutal. They'll pay for his defiance. I'll cut them open and pull out their guts and string them up from the buildings to die." Morgan raised his sword, the metal still dripping blood, and grinned. "Come home, you fools. Come home to die."

His words wafted out past the shore, born on an echo of magic rebounding through the air. A tiny wave adrift, to be snagged hours later and reeled in by another tendril of power, a line cast from the Lost Sea.

Then the eyes of gods turned towards Rock Island.

Twilight settled in as Morgan strode proudly along the docks, watching some of his men roll a few of the dead villagers off the docks into the harbour. The rest of his men were looting the village and destroying whatever they fancied to wreck. Morgan felt a sense of pride as he walked, careful not to slip in blood, and occasionally kicking at a body or stray limb.

"Aye. We done good work here." Morgan smiled.

Then behind him he heard a scraping noise and the breeze wafted the smell of decay to his nose. He stopped and turned around, his smile widening. The wind swayed the bodies strung up on the buildings, some dangling by their own intestines as well as rope. A few still moaned, clinging to life. Morgan chuckled at the faint sounds of the dead and dying, a warm tingle coursing through his skin.

"Admiring your deeds?" The Crow circled overhead before landing on a nearby pier post.

"Of course. Always take the time to bask in a deed well done. And this we did well, taking the village with nary an outcry or soul escaping. I sent some men back to the ships in a longboat and our fleet will be arriving soon. The harbour's deep enough for them to berth. By the time Captain Morrow arrives we'll be back aboard with our loot, ready to fight. As long as you send word like you promised." He gave the Crow a hard look.

"I will. You'll get your fight. I'll deliver the message. No doubt the repugnant visions of your handiwork will draw him here quickly."

"Repugnant!" Morgan's lip curled into a sneer. "You're not getting squeamish, are you, birdie? My flair in the killing not to your taste?"

The Crow ruffled his feathers and cawed. "How you

kill your fellow mortals is none of my affair. However, your macabre display of the dead with that awful stench and the scattered bits of flesh and fluids is quite repugnant."

Morgan laughed, doubling over in his amusement. "Oh, that's rich, birdie. A fastidious crow. Your lot being carrion birds. You should be feasting on those corpses, not complaining about the smell."

The Crow snapped his wings out, fluffed his feathers and screeched, "I am not one of those filthy carrion birds! Never call me that!" Shadows snaked out from the Crow's wingtips and Morgan stopped laughing as the tendrils wrapped around his throat. Emerald fire danced from Morgan's fingers and the pair glared at each other for several moments.

Finally Morgan croaked through the constriction around his throat. "Didn't mean any insult." The shadows withdrew and the Crow folded in his wings. Morgan quenched his magic as well. He asked, "We good, birdie?"

"I suppose." The Crow replied, both his body and his tone still ruffled.

Morgan grinned, ignored any remaining ill will and walked away. The Crow glared at him as he left. Then the Crow murmured to the wind and himself, "We may still need each other, you filthy pirate, but I won't forget this insult."

◆

"So, all is not well between the Crow and this pirate. That should help us." Reis spoke softly, his voice tired and cheerless. He laid a hand on his son's shoulder. "I'm sorry we didn't find out in time. Those poor villagers." Reis exhaled heavily. His hand fell back to his side. "It's difficult seeing that horror. I hope this is the last instance we need to check on those creatures."

Rafe let the scrying vision fade, even if the memories

of what he saw in Shell River would remain vividly etched in his thoughts. "Morgan always was a brutal bastard. I should have shredded his soul into a thousand pieces the first time." He clenched his jaw and his fingers curled into a fist.

Reis let out a soft sigh. "Take comfort in the fact he won't be so lucky this time. I talked to her, and she has agreed to take care of Morgan. She even agreed to wait for the navy to arrive unless the pirates decide to leave the village."

"Good." Rafe expelled a sigh of relief. "I wasn't sure she'd help. Or wait. During our regular updates, Pelham was adamant about the navy's involvement. He wants some of those pirates to hang. After we spotted Morgan sailing north, Pelham turned his fleet to the chase, but without knowing where..." Rafe stopped talking, regret eating at him.

If only I had seen more. Glimpses weren't enough. Not enough to head him off, see the route he sailed or his destination. Or warn the navy. Damn the Crow for hiding them from our eyes until it was too late.

Reis' voice cut into his thoughts, echoing them with his words. "No, the navy hadn't much of a chance to catch them, not with their ships concealed by magical means. And no way of intercepting them, not knowing their objective. They'll be part of it now though."

"The navy, yes. I'll update the Outer Islands fleet on Morgan's whereabouts." Rafe shook off his guilt. "Pelham will want to be there for the end."

"An odd man, Pelham." Reis seemed strangely amused. "You know Lynna's taken a liking to him? I wonder if she'll head to Rock Island with him?"

"Perhaps. And I am aware of her friendship, but I'd prefer not to discuss it." Rafe gave his father a warning glance. "Besides, we have important things to consider. Namely, the Crow. How do we separate him from Morgan and get him to the Lost Sea?"

"Ah, that. Not as large a problem as I had thought. You heard them. The Crow's coming to you. And if he holds true to form, it will be within your dreams. I suggest confronting him there and extending an invitation. If you goad him in the correct manner, the creature's ego will bring him right to this island."

Rafe smiled. "Now that I can do."

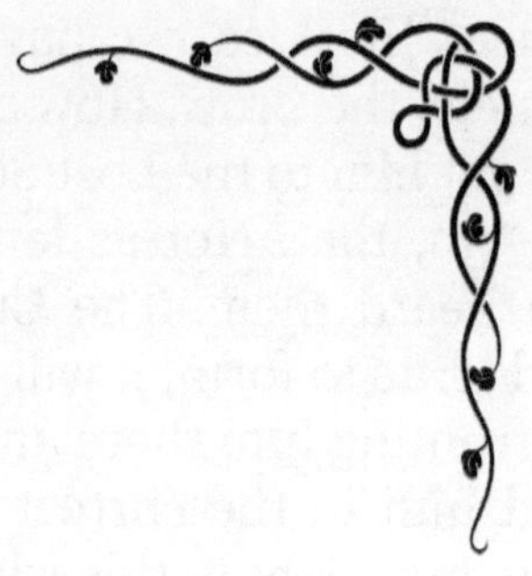

Chapter Nineteen
Shadows and Dreams

Asleep in his quarters on the *Celestial Jewel*, Rafe drifted slowly into a dream. His mind flowed past reality into a chimera, pieces of desire and longing clicking together to buoy up an illusion, to alight in an unreal space. The scent of warm ocean wind buffeted him, and he found himself on a beach, staring at an indistinct twilight horizon, pillows of mist floating across the sea.

His dream self took a breath, inhaling the fresh night air and the tang of the salt sea. For a moment he savoured the feeling of being alone. Of having no duties, no crew to oversee, no problems to solve. Only the beauty of the sea and sand to care about. He wanted to lie on the beach, feel the sand against his skin and watch the stars unfold in the sky overhead.

Until a strange flapping of wings told him he wasn't as alone as he presumed.

Rafe looked up, seeing the shape of a crow flying above him in the sky. He looked away, his gaze turning back out to sea. He waited. He heard the unnatural rustle of leaves behind him and felt the first strains of shadow magic creep into his dream. He whirled to face the Crow.

"No need for that." Rafe's voice echoed loudly and he stared at the Crow's invading eddies of gloom that infected his reverie. "I know why you are here, Nightmare Crow."

The Crow gave a low screech as he realized Rafe saw him and the swirling darkness surrounding the bird disappeared. He shifted on his branch and spread his wings as if to fly away.

"No need to flee." Rafe reached out a semblance of a hand. "And no need for deceit or tricks. I already know about Shell River. I saw the aftermath of what happened there." Rafe shuddered, the movement echoed by his sleeping form back on his ship.

"You saw?" The Crow tilted his head, puzzlement in his voice. "How?" And then, "That wasn't me. That was Morgan."

"I know." Rafe sighed. "I've dealt with his madness before. Death didn't improve his disposition. But he is of no consequence anymore. Steps have been taken to deal with him."

"Have they now?" The Crow chuckled. And then he hissed. "A step ahead of us, are you? So you're not coming to Rock Island?"

"No. I'm not the one coming. But someone you are very familiar with will see Morgan is stopped. It's your fate I want to discuss."

"Want me to give up, do you?" The Crow sneered. "Well I won't. If I can't lure you out, I'll steal Morgan's power and try again. We will face each other sooner or later, God of Souls!"

"I know." Rafe smiled. "I think sooner is best."

"What?" The Crow flapped his wings. "Wait. What are

you up to? What are you scheming?"

"No scheme." The lie tripped easily off his tongue. "This has been coming for a long time. Best if we stop playing these games and end it. Winner take all." Rafe grinned, a corner of his mouth crooking a bit higher than the other. "That's what you want, isn't it?"

"It is," the Crow warily replied. "But why should I believe you suddenly wish to face me? To hazard the fate of your precious world on one battle? That's reckless, even for you."

Rafe sighed. "That's where we are headed. You know it and I can see it. Why prolong the inevitable? And I'm tired of dealing with all your emissaries: my sisters, Ashetus, Morgan. Or were they the point? Are you too afraid to face me alone?"

"I'm not afraid!" The Crow waved his wings and the dream branch bounced under his antics.

"Then why do it at all? Why not come at me directly?" Inward Rafe took delight at goading the creature.

"I may not be afraid, but neither am I a fool." The Crow cawed. "I do what I must. And I never wanted to involve you in any of this. But as you said, it has come down to us. I need you, your power, to accomplish my goal."

"Do you now?" Rafe's voice sounded amused.

"Who else would do, but the great God of Souls." The Crow gave a caw, almost a laugh. "Three games, God of Souls, three times we played. Dancing around the King and Queen, around Ulerne and Death." The Crow moved his wings. "The first match went to you. The second to me. So perhaps you are correct. It is time for the endgame."

"It is. Yet, was it all necessary? All the dead, all the strife?" Rafe chose his next words carefully, trying to draw out information. "What do you want? What does all this accomplish? All your efforts seem rather pointless to me."

"Do they?" A soft cackle sounded. "So little you see. Win or lose the goal was always about power. Stealing magic. The first game was for your death or hers. Pit the God of Souls against the Goddess of the Moon and then collect the spoils." The Crow stretched out his wings, a touch of pride in his voice. "Do you know what happens when a god dies?"

Rafe nodded.

"Of course you do. Most every non-mortal creature does. Power floods the world, waiting to be stolen." The Crow sighed. "I truly thought she might kill you, and I could take your power for myself, save myself the trouble of tricking you or destroying you. Then I expected you to kill your sister. What a feast that would have been. The offspring of the stars and Death." The bird sighed and ruffled its feathers. "But you did not. So I contented myself on the scraps of her fattened children as they died, draining their leftover magic with each final breath. Not enough, not enough; your sister gained the most of it. But I took what I could and moved on."

Rafe looked at him, a puzzled thought forming. "So if your goal was my death, my power, why try to destroy the After World?"

"Still for the power. To drain that realm's energy as it died. And to get her attention. To draw Death from her hiding place." The bird rasped and glared. "I hate her, you know."

Rafe raised an eyebrow. "She can have that effect on those who know her. What did she do to you?"

"Many things." The Crow then hesitated as if wanting to say more, finishing with, "Mostly, she took my brothers after they died. I wanted them back. Needed them. Too bad it didn't work." The Crow clacked his beak.

"I'm quite happy it didn't work." Rafe grunted. "You

still haven't told me why. Why do you need all this power? Are you that greedy for magic? It can't simply be about returning to the Realm of the Stars."

"Of course it's about returning there! There is nothing more important to me." The Crow clacked his beak in anger. "How dare you think this is about greed? I have no lust for magic. It is merely a means to an end." The Crow raised his head and drew in his wings. "I want back what was stolen from me. By your family. By Ulerne."

Rafe let out a hiss. "Is this revenge? Punishment for what you believe my grandfather did to you?"

"Your grandfather deserves punishment!" The Crow shrieked. "He stole from me! He betrayed me! My brothers died for him! And he walked away! He didn't care! We were his family and he didn't care!"

The bird fluffed out his feathers and spread his wings. He lowered his voice, his tone becoming almost pensive. "We argued after... I was angry, said things..." The Crow's voice cracked, his words trailing off. Then he blurted, "But he shouldn't have left me." He tilted his head. "Your grandfather was careless, heartless. He ran from the consequences of his actions." The Crow sighed. "Still, I forgave him. Yet, he never forgave me. He punished me for my anger. Trapped me here in this insubstantial world, locked me in this pitiable body!" The Crow shook his wings. "He stole my true form! That was the worst betrayal!" A slight sheen of tears formed in the Crow's eyes. "But I forgave him."

"It doesn't sound like it."

"Maybe not to you!" The Crow puffed out feathers and spread his wings. "But I did! I did! I only ever wanted what I had before. The Realm of the Stars, Ulerne, my brothers. If Death had given me back my brothers..." The Crow's voice softened into a whisper and the words faded. "If she had, I wouldn't have needed to steal power. Without them... I can't do it without them unless I take magic from other sources." The Crow looked directly at Rafe. "Sources like you. You can send me home, back to the Realm of the Stars. No more schemes, no more trouble. Send me back and I am gone forever."

Rafe exhaled and replied, his tone gentle, "I cannot. I wish I could, but you don't belong there. It upset the balance between realms, the Shadow Birds in the Realm of the Stars. You cannot go back." Rafe shook his head, casting his eyes downward. "You can stay here. Perhaps even in your true form if that is what you wish."

"No." The Crow hissed and drew in his wings. "You lie. I can go back. I can see the stars again. I will see the stars again."

Rafe looked up. "If that is your answer, then we are enemies. But we can, at least, stop these games."

The Crow tilted his head. "What do you have in mind?"

"A showdown. Near the Gateway between realms, at the island temple. Just the two of us, winner takes the power." Rafe smiled. "That is what you wanted? The chance to steal my magic and gain the power to open the Gateway back to the Realm of the Stars."

The Crow nodded. "Or force you to open it. Either way."

"Well, I'm offering the opportunity to try. No more games, no more pirates or pawns. Only the God of Souls versus the Nightmare Crow."

The Crow remained still, his eyes glittering in the dream light. "I accept. I tire of these games anyway. Three days from now. Agreed?"

"Agreed."

The mist of the dream began to swirl and the Crow spread his wings as if to leave, but asked one more question. "What of Morgan and his pirates? Should I take care of them?"

Rafe shook his head. "Leave them to me. In two days, he will be no one's problem."

The Crow chuckled. "It would be my pleasure."

A wave of mist flowed across the space between the two, and then the dream faded to black, with Rafe waking up in his bed aboard the *Celestial Jewel*.

Chapter Twenty
Battling Pirates

High above the shores of Rock Island, shadows gathered in the sky and the Nightmare Crow flew back into the world from the realm of dreams. He circled over the trees and beaches, over the pirate ships and the now rotting settlement of Shell River. He finally descended, landing on the roof of an outlying harbour building.

Night had settled in and the Crow saw lights on the pirate ships as well as illumination from the village and the sounds of carousing men singing off-key. He cawed and hissed.

"No doubt the fools are getting drunk." He waggled his wings in disgust and turned his attention back to the ships. He took a breath and flew away, headed to the *Shadow Raider*.

He found Morgan on the quarterdeck, swilling rum and staring at the stars. Two pirates were sprawled on the deck at his feet, empty bottles beside their snoring bodies. Another man sat against the helm, counting a bag of coins, while others danced on the main deck. As the Crow landed on the rail, he noticed a severed head hung from a mast and Finn batted at it with a belaying pin.

"Has your murderous little protégé invented a new game?" The Crow flicked a wing in the direction of Finn.

Morgan greeted him with an "Oh, yer back, are ye?" and swallowed some rum. Then added, "Aye. Finn's havin' some fun. Tha' boy's a delight." He waved the bottle at the Crow, who shuffled out of the way of the swinging glass object. "Bloody lot of 'em is havin' fun. Drinkin'. Drinkin' is fun."

"Yes, I'm sure." The Crow glared, but Morgan didn't notice.

"So, birdie. Did ya do yer business? He's comin'?" Morgan turned and leaned towards the rail, his face inches from the Crow.

The bird drew in his wings and clacked his beak. "Yes. I did what needed to be done. You'll have your reckoning. In a day or two."

"Hurrah!" Morgan raised his bottle and downed several gulps of the liquor, rum dribbling down his chin. "To the end of Captain Morrow." He swallowed another dram of rum.

"Indeed." The Crow replied with nothing more, leaving Morgan to his bottle, and flew into the sky.

❖

When morning dawned, the Crow returned to the *Shadow Raider* with the sun's first light. A foul-tempered Morgan growled at his lethargic crew and rubbed at his temples. The Crow landed on the ship's wheel and pecked at the shoulder of the helmsman that slumped against his station. The man waved at the bird angrily and the Crow flew to the rail.

In a laughing voice, the bird asked, "Is this how you

will defeat the great Captain Morrow? A hung-over bunch of pirates against a god?"

"What? What're you blathering on about, birdie?" Morgan scowled.

"The imminent arrival of the enemy, good pirate." The Crow openly chuckled. "As I informed you last evening."

"What?" Morgan roared the word. "He's actually coming?"

The Crow bobbed his head. "Soon you will have your reckoning."

"Damnation and sea spit!" Headache seemingly forgotten and in full anger, Morgan yelled at his crew, "Get your lily-livered carcasses to work! Prepare the ship for battle! Get the signal flags working and inform the other ships! We got ourselves a god to kill!"

The Crow flapped a wing, catching Morgan's attention. "I'll leave you to it then, Captain. I have things of my own to prepare."

Morgan nodded with a slight grimace. "Aye. I expect ye do. Setting out to drain the power of a god takes work, I imagine."

"It does." The bird chuckled and leapt to the sky. He circled the ships before flying along the shoreline and up towards the clouds. As he travelled he murmured, "Poor Morgan. You won't be facing our Captain Morrow. But I will. Far, far away from here." The bird turned and banked, heading out to the open sea.

◆

Morgan stalked the deck, pacing, anger simmering after waiting two days with neither the God of Souls nor the Crow in sight. He mumbled and muttered as he walked, "Birdie best not have lied to me, or I'll fricassee his hide. That's right, roasted crow over a spit, with a side helping of his guts in butter."

Morgan made another circuit of the quarterdeck, both Finn and the helmsman avoiding eye contact with the pirate. Cooped up on the ship, maintaining a magical fog spell to shield their ships from easy notice had made Morgan frustrated and restless, and ready to skewer the first man who looked at him funny. Two poor souls had fresh wounds from such encounters already and no man wanted to be number three.

"Where is he! Rafe Morrow, where the hell are ye! Come face me, coward! And bring that lying feathered crow with ye!" Morgan screamed his rage at the world, his words echoing out over the waters.

All chatter stopped on the *Shadow Raider* and a hush settled. It seemed as if even the birds and island wildlife quieted and a blanket of overwrought silence fell across both the pirates and the remains of Shell River.

Then a frantic cry came from the edge of the harbour, from the farthest pirate vessel. "Ships! We have ships coming in fast." A similar cry came from another ship on the opposite side, "Heading from the west too! More ships!"

"What!" Morgan shouted, and pulled out a spyglass, raising it to view the horizon as a roaring boom broke over the ships. He heard someone shriek, "Cannon fire!" As he frantically searched with the spyglass, he saw telltale wisps of smoke, and the unmistakable ships of the navy filled his vision. More booms sounded to each side, and then the sound rebounded from the front. He spun to see the looming sight of ships bearing down on the *Shadow Raider*.

"Position the ship to return fire, you fools! Fire the damned cannon!" He gave the order, but he knew it was too late. Somehow he'd been tricked and the trap sprung. He let the magic holding the fog in place go. No use in hiding any more; the enemy knew they were here.

He ground his teeth, enough fight in him to try to get his ship into position to volley back and trade fire, even as his stomach churned in fear. He saw his other ships get slammed with the navy's superior weapons, watched them list and take on water. He listened to his men's screams and knew there would be no escape for his fledgling fleet. Morgan also knew, as the navy ships continued to blast their cannon, he had been betrayed. He roared his rage at the skillful ambush: bottled in the harbour with nowhere to run. He glanced at his fleet, now with one ship sinking, another listing, and facing an overwhelming enemy. They'd never manoeuvre quickly enough for the ships to use their own cannons against the navy.

"Time to leave." He whispered softly, "Time to abandon ship and crew. This captain ain't going down with his ship."

He leaned back, one hand on the rail and repeated his previous order. "Get us turned broadside, so we can return fire!" As his men's attention turned to duty and the ship, he summoned his magic, his body alight in a green glow.

The helmsman glanced back. Morgan held a breath, but the man simply said, "Fixing to do something to them, Captain?" At Morgan's nod, he turned his face away and Morgan let out the breath. The pirate waited a few moments, to make certain all eyes were elsewhere, and then leapt over the stern's rail, whispering one word.

"Chydfane."

Morgan glided in the air, but didn't fall, slowly descending to the waters of the harbour on a sizzling flame of energy. Then he skimmed across the surface, his feet making ripples, until he landed on the docks of Shell River. Behind him he heard the faint cries and shouts of his men, and the boom of the navy cannon. He dashed forward, glancing back once to see another ship begin to sink and a cannonball smash into the bow of the *Shadow Raider*.

"Damn bastards." He hissed through his teeth and ran, heading along the street of the village, planning to backtrack to where the longboats were still stashed.

He only made it as far as the ridge above the village. There, as he stopped for a breath, the air darkened and a black, thin form stepped out of the shadows. For the first time since his resurrection Morgan felt vulnerable. Green fire snapped from his fingers and with a snarl, Morgan fired a blast of green flame at his adversary.

Death caught the edge of his attack in mid-air and swirled it around her arm. It hovered there for a moment before she took a deep breath, inhaled the flame and swallowed the magic. She licked her lips and then looked at Morgan. "Death magic? Truly? Did you think that would stop me?"

Morgan choked out a cry of dread, turned tail and ran for his life. His legs pumped, feet smacking and slipping against the stone and grass, his heart beating a rapid thump inside his chest. His breath came in gasps, and whimpers escaped his throat as he raced, blindly fleeing a god no one could escape. His thoughts churned with anger, resentment, and feelings of betrayal, chased by a fear of dying, or worse, being adrift as a ghost once more. He pushed himself, racing the inevitable until his muscles ached, until his legs stumbled and he fell, tumbling along the ground, gathering bruises and scrapes. He rose to his knees to see the shadows coalesce in front of him, and a black figure reached for him.

Death grabbed him under the chin with a strong, bony hand, and dug her fingers into his face. She lifted his head and her eyes seemed to bore into his. Morgan screamed. Death smiled.

"Black Axe Morgan. Mine at last." Death chuckled.

"First, I will take back that stolen magic of yours. Neither you nor that necromancer deserved my gift."

Her fingers tightened on his face and her other hand came up and forced his mouth open. Death leaned in, placed her mouth on his, and inhaled. Morgan's body shook violently, erupting in green flame. Then slowly, with each breath she took, Death siphoned away all of Morgan's magical energy. When she finished, she let the pirate go and he collapsed to his hands and knees, gagging and spewing bile.

He tried to crawl away, still retching, but Death gave him a kick, flopping him onto his back like a beached fish. "I'm not done with you yet, Morgan." Death loomed over him, a taunting look on her face.

Morgan raised an arm, as if to ward her off, and cried, "Mercy. Have mercy on me. I only served ya with me killing. Sent you souls. I spent me life serving Death."

She stood there, staring, her cloak and shadows swirling in the wind. "True. You do worship Chaos and Death. But I am no fool you can trick with empty words. You served only your own ego and pleasure, not me or my mother. Yet, your own demise will serve me well. For an eternity." Death knelt down and placed a hand on Morgan's face. He flinched and shivered as she said, "This will not be painless or quick. You will suffer." She stroked his skin, and then her hand lifted above his head.

Death's shadows slithered from her fingers and wrapped around his throat, snaked into his ears and mouth, pierced his eyeballs, and twisted about his torso and limbs. Dark, rotating barbs punctured his flesh, stabbing deep into his blood and bone. Morgan shrieked, a sound echoing the horror of his victims, reflecting their pain and torture. His body shook in spasms, his back arching, his body flailing against his restraints. Then, inch by inch, second by ticking second, Death sucked away his life, removing his soul from his body in tiny bits to her realm. She stood over him for an hour, watching him scream, then moan, then whimper as his voice dried and faded. She watched his body wither and shrink while his skin shrivelled, his bones cracked and turned to powder. His blood congealed, his organs contracted, his eyes desiccated in their sockets, he regurgitated and thrashed on the ground. Yet, he remained alive through it all, through all the agony, until the last small fragment of his soul came to Death. Then, and only then, did Black Axe Morgan die, his dried-out corpse staring at the sky with hollow eye sockets.

Death chuckled, vanishing in a swirl of inky black haze.

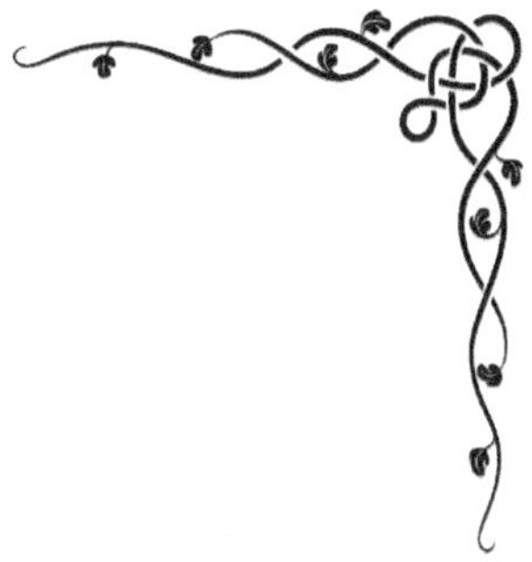

Chapter Twenty-One
A Pirate's End

The navy ships anchored at the harbour entrance, effectively blockading the port and village of Shell River. Two pirate ships had been scuttled, and another, the *Shadow Raider,* listed heavily to her right side. Drowned pirates and bodies of the crews broken from cannon shot washed up on shore with the change of the tide, their wretched second life ended more permanently than the first.

Most of the surviving pirates were now locked in the brigs of the navy ships, but a few, including Finn, had jumped overboard from their vessels and swum to freedom. Patrols scoured the countryside tracking the fugitives. One by one, they were hauled into custody. Finn they found by Morgan's body, the youth weeping over the corpse of his fallen mentor. He struggled and shouted as the navy sailors yanked him to his feet and clapped shackles on his wrists.

"You bastards! What did you do to him? How did you

bastards kill the great Black Axe Morgan?"

One naval man glanced at the corpse, shuddering. "That's Morgan? Bad way to go, even for what he did, but that weren't us. Your captain messed with gods, laddy. They did this." He nodded at the remains. Finn sagged, his head slouched, and let himself be carted off into custody. The sailors brought him to the docks, where he heard the sounds of hammers and saw the sight of several makeshift gallows being erected on the shore.

One of the navy men grinned as they walked past, and said, "They're for you and the rest of your fellow scum. Soon we will slip a noose over that filthy neck of yours and hoist you up to hang for your crimes."

Another man spat at Finn. "Hanging's too good for the likes of you. Should be gutted and roasted on a spit."

Yet another sailor chimed in, "Slice him like they did that lady, and toss him to the razor fish. I'd wager the goddess wouldn't save this one." The navy men all laughed and hauled Finn into a longboat with two other captured pirates. Then they rowed back to their ships and locked the prisoners in the brig.

Finn sat in a corner, wallowing in grief, waiting for the end.

<hr>

A day later, navy sailors led a shackled Finn to a rocky beach, parading him underneath the shadow of the gallows framework. He knew he had been the first chosen for execution and he took perverse pride in it. Finn didn't flinch as the rope went around his neck and the appointed executioner tightened the knot. The man stepped away and shouted, "He's ready, boys, hoist him up!"

Finn heard the squeak of the pulleys and the grunts of the men, and the rope tightened around his neck, slicing off his breath. He felt his body rise and his feet flail in open air. He thrashed in fear as the rope kept contracting, choking him, squeezing his life away slowly. His actions only hastened the strangulation, his breath cut off into short burning gasps and his head pounding as the rope restricted his blood supply. His vision dimmed into hazy pinpricks of light and shadow while pain sliced through him. He felt heat in his groin with something wet dripping down his legs and heard a shout of, "He's pissed himself, boys!" as he prayed for it to end.

Finn welcomed his mind sinking into unconsciousness, ready to accept his demise, but he didn't die. He hung there for hours—as did many of his fellow pirates after him—the rope digging into his neck, throttling his breath, but his heart still thumped in his chest. His life still tethered to the world and his body.

The first words Finn heard after the navy cut him down were, "Damn necromancer!" He opened his eyes and saw Pelham scowling down at him. He tried to speak, but only a croaking sound came out, and his throat burned as if it was on fire.

Pelham spat on him and barked an order. "Haul that scum to his feet!" Two sailors hopped to obey, dragging Finn up.

Pelham sneered. "I suppose you're wondering why you're still alive. Apparently, whatever the damned sorcerer did to you makes you impervious to certain types of death. Like hanging." Pelham grinned at the relief and surprise on Finn's face.

"You like that news, do you? Well don't get used to it. It only means we have to start over. You're still being executed. And in a more fitting way, if you ask me." Pelham paused, savouring the fear creeping back into Finn's expression. "Every one of you degenerate pirates will have to be beheaded."

Finn tried to whimper, but no sound came from his damaged throat. He struggled to escape as the sailors dragged him away. A few well-placed blows subdued him, and they led Finn to the docks to meet his fate. Pelham followed, wanting to see the execution.

A stern-faced man stood at the edge of a wharf, holding a great two-handed sword. The sailors hauled Finn to his side and pushed him to his knees. Pelham came forward and addressed the pirate. "You're lucky. One of our navy crewmen is from Resmar. He uses their blades and can wield it with skill. He'll take your head off cleanly if you don't try to evade the blow or struggle. It'll be a quick and relatively painless death, more than you gave to your victims. If you resist... Well, it will mostly likely be bloody and messy. My advice is to close your eyes and accept what's coming."

Finn glanced around at the naval sailors and officers surrounding him, at the tide of angry faces and armed men. He nodded, resigned to his end, but didn't close his eyes. He stared at Pelham with one last bit of defiance, as the man stepped away, out of range of the blood splatter. Finn's gaze followed him, as the swish of the blade sliced through the air and across Finn's neck. His head came off in one clean blow and hit the docks, bouncing and rolling to a stop by Pelham's feet. The naval commander resisted the urge to kick it into the harbour.

Instead he relayed an order. "Clean up this corpse and load it into a burial box. Then bring the next prisoner for execution."

Sailors gave an "aye, sir," and Finn's remains were carted away. At the other end of the docks, a wail broke along the wind as another man was dragged forward to pay for his crimes.

Chapter Twenty-Two
Death and the Pirate

Death waited in her realm, sitting on her throne made from the bones and sinew of creatures long dead and rotted, and the echoing screams of shadows. At her feet sat her new toy: the soul of Black Axe Morgan. He curled in a ball, whimpering, hoping she would forget his existence. He always thought his death would be the end, not the beginning of an eternity of torment.

"I am not a patient creature, Morgan. I don't like being relegated to an observer." Death whipped a shadow through his spectral eyeball and twisted his head around so it faced backwards. Excruciating agony shot through his soul and he screamed.

Death smiled. "So nice of you to try to cheer my mood. Such delightful screams you have." Another shadow snaked out and twisted his arm. Death was rewarded with another scream. She settled back on her throne, her mood mollified. "At least I can amuse myself while I wait for my son to take action."

Morgan moaned as she reeled his essence in closer. She pulled his head around to face her, laughing at his shrieks. Then she reached out and snapped off the ghostly tip of his left pinky finger while he watched and begged her to stop. Death ignored his pleas, inhaled the energy that she held and consumed that small morsel of his soul.

"Tasty. You have a slight bitter and dark flavour, Mr. Morgan." She let him fall, and he crawled away to whimper.

Death chuckled at his antics, continuing to muse aloud. "I used to rule this world, you know. Walk the gloom that enveloped everything. I travelled over the land, the sea, through the sky. Everything was mine, and all who lived here bowed before my presence, trembled at my coming. I threw it all away for a chance to love." She sighed, like the opening of a grave. "And do you know, Morgan, I would do it again. I may sit here, waiting for my son to reap the consequences of that foolish love, but I do not regret it. I miss it, I am angered by it, I would scream its name to a thousand souls and weep its end, but I do not regret the feeling." She stared at Morgan. "Do you think that odd, mortal?"

Morgan gawked, not answering.

Death sighed. "I expect you do. Mortals regret many things. Especially broken love. More than gods, I think." She tilted her head with the creak of bones. "Do you have regrets, pirate?" She looked at Morgan, who stared back, terrified, still not speaking. Death chuckled, continuing her musings. "Of course you do, you are here with me. No doubt you regret every inch of your black heart."

She rose from her throne and walked over to Morgan, who visibly cringed. She knelt, crooning softly, "Would you change your fate if you could? Do you think your black heart could have been redeemed, pirate?"

Morgan trembled, but croaked, "Yes, I wish I could

change my fate, but redemption? Men like me don't change our hearts."

Death hissed, not liking the answer. She reached out to strike him, but stayed her hand, only asking, "And what of creatures that are not men? Ones born of shadows and night? What of the Nightmare Crow? Can he be saved?"

For a moment, anger dispelled the fear in Morgan and without a thought of caution he spat out, "That deceitful betraying bastard? His heart is colder and darker than mine. He'll never change!" And a second after the words left his mouth, the terror returned, as Death snarled, her bony fingers reaching for his face.

Yet, again, she did nothing. Her icy grip hovered over his face, and then she moved her hand away. She sat down beside Morgan and smiled at him. A shiver shook his form.

"You are right. He is deceitful. He will betray. He was always so; a selfish creature. When he lies you believe him, even if you know the truth. But he is loyal as well, in his own way. When he loves, he is magnificent. And he was mine, once."

A strangled sound came from Morgan, a half-gurgle, half-gasp.

Death laughed. "I know. A very strange pair we made. Yet, we loved each other. Or I thought we did. Love is not an easy thing to hold. Perhaps it was a lie, perhaps it wasn't. But the connection is still there. I still feel it. I still see the Shadow Bird I knew under the Nightmare Crow." She sighed. "Yet, here I sit with you, waiting for my son to destroy my love." Death laid a finger on Morgan's face and turned his head so their eyes met. "So, I ask you, pirate with the blackened heart. Should I remain here and do nothing, or give my love another chance to come back to me?"

"You're asking me 'bout love?" Surprise chased fear

from Morgan's thoughts. "I ain't never loved no one but meself." He hesitated before adding, "But if I ever did, and was in yer shoes, I'd want to know where I stood. Take the chance."

"Why?" Death tilted her head, curious. "Why poke at the old wounds?"

Morgan smiled. "Them wounds of yours don't need poking, they're still fresh. And all that wondering of yourn is going to keep 'em that way. Wondering makes you imagine the worst, not the good."

"Does it?" Death sighed. "Perhaps, but what if the worst is true?"

Morgan grunted. "Then you'd know. You ain't sitting there dithering anymore."

"But how to know?" Death mumbled, "How to know? Memories are deceivers, are they not?"

"Why don't you just ask the bastard?"

"I..." Death smiled, "Yes, why don't I just ask him?" Death reached out and Morgan cringed, but she simply patted his head as if he was a dog. "Most excellent advice, my pirate. Indeed, I shall ask my Crow."

Death rose to her feet and in a swirl of shadows she vanished.

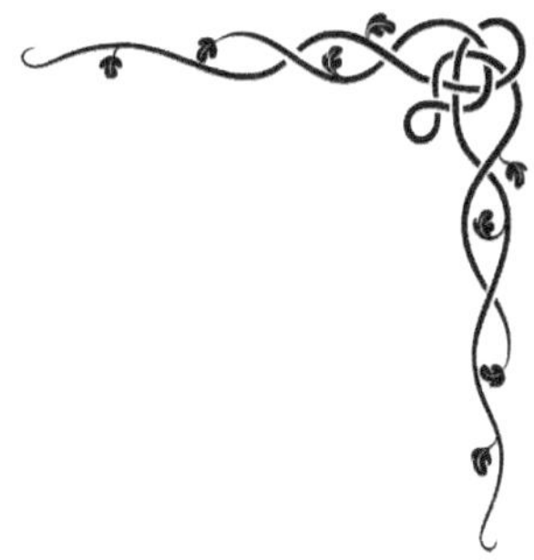

Chapter Twenty-Three
Sanctuary

The morning sun rose over Rotter's Bay, its light sparkling over the water like precious gems. High in the trees, the Crow roused from his night's sleep and flew down to a certain spot on the beach. He scratched a rune in the soft sand with the tip of a wing and chuckled.

"You'll be waiting, God of Souls, at the temple, but I'll be coming through the Gateway. I know you have schemes and traps, for all your words, but I have some of my own."

The Crow closed his eyes, the flesh under his feathers rippling. Shadows gathered around him, inky black mist summoned from a once eternal night, and underneath, an emerald spark, twice stolen from men now dead.

He opened his eyes, letting a spark of green-tinted fire slither down his wing, lighting his feathers in energy. He touched the magic to the sand and watched with glee as the rune illuminated with the transferred energy. He stepped back and waited.

The air shimmered and warped and—as it had

before—a portal doorway appeared on the beach. The Crow peered through, checking to see the other side remained a clearing empty of gods. Satisfied no one waited for him, he leapt into the air and flew through to the unnamed island in the Lost Sea. Behind him the Gateway closed, and only a slightly shimmering obelisk remained to mark his passing. The Crow flew onward, over the temple to a spot on the far side of the island.

The Gateway's opening did not go unnoticed. A shimmer of energy resonated inside the temple. Rafe and his father glanced at each other.

Reis sighed. "He's arrived. Ever the deceiver, that creature."

Rafe shrugged. "We knew he wouldn't come as we agreed. He doesn't trust me and I don't trust him. It won't matter, his deceit won't avail him a thing."

"Still, I wonder what he is planning." Reis' words faded into a hint of breeze wandering through the cracks in the walls and fled into the great sky above the island. And across that sky, the Crow swooped down to land in a small clearing.

The creature brushed a wingtip over the ground. The grass shivered under his touch. The Crow smiled. "It's still here. Good." He folded his wings and whispered, "*Dagu Iwch.*"

The grass before him wilted, turning brown and shrivelling into dust to be blown away on the wind. Etched in the dirt, a rune glowed red. It pulsed and hummed, waiting. The Crow stretched out a foot and stepped on the magic symbol.

A thrum sounded and the earth shivered. The air above the rune quivered and rent like tearing fabric, spilling out a crimson light before shifting and morphing into a portal doorway. The Crow stepped through and found himself in a small underground room. The door snapped shut behind him, changing into a dirt and stone wall.

The Crow looked around. Nothing had been disturbed in the decade since he had last been here. He remembered when he first found the spot, well before Reis moved the island, but after Ulerne abandoned him. He stumbled on it by accident, a tiny rift between dimensions. It hadn't taken much to widen it, to create a sanctuary and hide it from the rest of the world. It had been his place to escape from the world until Reis stole it away.

"But I found you again, didn't I, when the necromancer first allowed me back on the island. He never knew, silly man. But then, he trusted me."

The Crow padded across the carved floor until he reached the centre. He stared at the symbols etched on the stone beneath his feet. Three days he worked to inscribe them into the essence of this place until he achieved the perfect arrangement. Here he could travel the dream corridors with ease, see beyond the limited vision left to him by Ulerne. Here he could be something close to what he used to be, to be Dream Walker and Shadow Bird again. If only...

The Crow sighed. "It would have been easier. Having this place. Not taken me centuries to come to this reckoning. In these last decades, here, I have done more, seen more than... But no use in wishing. I'm here now. Ready to win."

He touched a clawed toe to a symbol, filling it with a drop of magic, and then on to another symbol, and another, and another, stepping and hopping to weave the spell he needed. Finally, he came back to the centre, connecting everything together.

He checked that the symbols were correct, drew his wings to his body and lowered his head. He dug his claws into the stone and felt the pulse of magic racing against the floor.

"Agr Yffordd. Gadwych mefynd mewyn."

At his raspy words the floor lit in a scarlet light and the radiance began to spin. Along the walls, images appeared: Llansfoot, Crickwell Island, Rock Island Temple, the Stone Fire Islands, the Archipelago of Nightfall, Raven Rock, Cataclysm Reef. And finally, images from the island above him: the temple, the Gateway and the *Celestial Jewel* anchored in the harbour.

The Crow gasped. "He's here? All along? Oh clever Death, sending him where you need him to be, protecting the Gateway. Well, it won't work. Won't work. It will only make it simpler."

The Crow hopped a step and moved two more, adding three more symbols to his pattern. One more and then another until he stood at the edge of the floor.

"Agr Twyidor."

For a moment, absolute silence settled and not a breath of time moved in the room. Then, on an opposite wall, stones shifted into a new configuration. Red light sparked between cracks and a yawning maw of darkness opened in the wall.

The Crow smiled at the entrance to the Dream World, watching its infinite space swirl and snap. He walked across the room, spread his wings and flew into its shadowy interior.

"And so it begins, God of Souls," the Crow whispered as the portal closed behind him.

***

Hours later, back from the Dream World and perched on a low branch in a tree, the Nightmare Crow chuckled to himself, satisfied he missed nothing, that his plan was sound. Every step was in place, his snare perfectly prepared.

"The seed of your destruction is waiting, God of Souls." He chuckled again and let out a contented sigh. "Soon, I'll have what I want. I'll be going home."

"The Realm of the Stars is not your home. Your home is with me." To the left of the tree, shadows coalesced and Death materialized. The Crow screeched and cawed repeatedly.

"Not now! Not when I'm so close! You cannot stop me!" He flew into the sky and circled her black-cloaked form.

Death looked up, shaking her head at his antics. "I'm not here to fight. Or to stop whatever you are planning. Settle down. I'm simply here to talk."

Suspicious, the Crow circled her twice more, before landing on a higher branch and glaring at her. "When did you decide you want to talk to me? Not try to hurt me?"

Death shrugged. "Perhaps I have mellowed over the centuries. Perhaps I miss you."

"You miss me?" His words dripped past an incredulous tone, and the Crow flapped his wings in surprise. Then he hissed. "What trickery are you weaving, Goddess?"

Death looked up at her former paramour. "No tricks. As I said, I just came to talk. About lost love. Forgiveness. Redemption." She danced a shadow around her finger. "There are things I would like to know."

The Crow shifted along his branch, hiding in among the leaves of the tree. His voice drifted from behind the foliage. "What things? And why now?" Another hiss, and then, "Does the God of Souls know you're here? Do you come to *plead* for him? Your words will not save him. I will not be any more merciful to him than I was to our son."

"Do not talk to me about Ashetus! Not after what you did!" Death's roar shook the tree and the ground, and leaves fell from the Crow's hiding place, revealing his feathered head and yellow eyes. The bird raised his wings as if ready to fly.

"Wait!" Death took a breath, stirring dust, and calmed her temper. The Crow folded his wings. "I did not come here for my son. Either son." She glared, but continued. "Morrannan does not know I am here, and whatever occurs between you two is your fate. I will not interfere." She paused, and for a second it seemed time stopped, then resumed. "But I am here to offer another path, and for you to answer questions."

"Questions?" The Crow leaned his head out slightly. "What questions do you have for me? You, of all creatures, know me, and my motivations."

"I do. I know you well, save for one thing." A sigh escaped her and a few leaves from the trees crumbled to dust. "Did you ever love me? Or did you lie, pretend the part to appease me?"

The Crow flapped his wings and replied, shock in his voice. "You doubt that? Doubt I loved you?"

Death nodded.

The Crow flew down to a lower branch, staring straight into Death's face. "I loved you. That was never the reason I left. It was—was..." He bowed his head, mumbling the next words, "Love wasn't enough. I saw the stars in someone's dreams, and then love wasn't enough."

"Oh, my poor Shadow Bird." Death reached out and stroked his feathers. "The stars were never for the likes of us. Forget your quest, this pursuit to return to the Realm of the Stars. Come with me, back to the night. Come home to your family."

The Crow lifted his head, and for a moment a sheen of tears dusted his eyes. Then he jerked his head and turned his back to Death. "I cannot. I will not. I will see the stars again."

The Crow leapt into the sky, soaring towards the clouds. In a flash of magic he disappeared into the darkness between worlds.

A sigh and a rattle rose from Death's throat as she watched him leave. "So be it, my love. I leave you to your fate." She disappeared in a black mist of gloom and bitterness and lingering sorrow.

Back in her realm, Death stalked across her terrain, headed to her throne to brood. She kicked Morgan as she passed him before sitting upon the bones of the fallen.

"My poor, poor Crow. You will never see the stars. Now you will have to face my son." She scowled at Morgan, who covered his head and cowered. Death laughed.

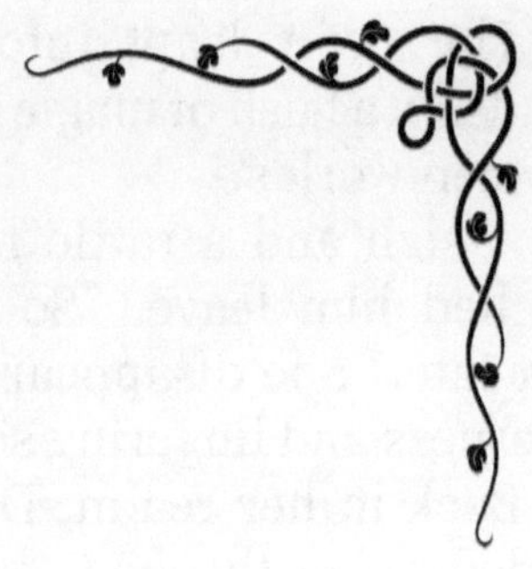

Chapter Twenty-Four
Dream World

Rafe stood in the underground chamber, the air surrounding him still and heavy in silence. His father waited in the temple, a god of last resort if he failed. Doubt warred with confidence in his thoughts. The treachery of the Crow worried him and he knew some scheme or trap awaited him, but he had his own trick to spring.

Time to commence.

Rafe inhaled, and magic sparked off his fingers. He flicked the energy against the walls and columns, spinning it around the room, opening the pathways, searching until he found the Crow. The images of the bird flickered in the dark space connecting existence, and the creature huddled there, alone.

"What are you up to, Crow?"

The bird turned his head as if he knew Rafe had spoken and Rafe heard a soft chuckle.

"So, it begins, does it?" Rafe whispered, a gentle challenge in the infinite space.

"It does." An answer echoed back, along with a screeching caw. The Crow dipped his head before taking flight. He flew straight at Rafe, shattering through the veil between places and soared straight into the chamber. He circled overhead and then settled to perch on a column.

"Well, well, such an interesting place." The Crow tilted his head, his voice sounding muffled. "Tucked away from prying eyes. A hidden scrying room within the temple, all these years. Clever. Reis' doing?"

Rafe nodded. "My father has many secrets. All leading us here."

"True." The Crow bobbed his head. "I admire your father, you know. A god of insight. He and I have that in common—thinking ahead, making plans. It pays to play the long game."

The Crow opened his beak and quickly spat out a glowing red seed. It spun downward and hit the floor, shattering. Tendrils of glowing red magic slithered across the chamber and formed a web of energy. The room snapped in sparks and raw power as if inside a storm. A wave of vertigo hit Rafe as all the pathways in the chamber shifted and redirected their reality.

The Crow spread his wings, shouting, "Your father's not the only one with secrets!" He took flight, laughing, and snatched at a thread of crimson light, yanking the magic along behind him in a circle. Rafe spun, another ripple of dizziness hitting him, and the world around them dissolved. For a few moments Rafe fought to keep his footing until his surroundings stabilized. He found himself elsewhere, in a barren plane, staring at the Crow perched in a dead tree.

He took a breath and exhaled. "Your trap is sprung, then?"

The Crow clacked his beak. "You knew?"

"I did." Rafe grinned.

"It won't matter." The Crow cawed, fanning his wings. "Welcome to the Dream World. Welcome to my domain."

"The Dream World?"

The Crow chuckled. "Yes. My domain. Long lost to change and time, but it never went away. It is part of everywhere and part of me. It is the source of my power."

In the distance something howled, someone laughed, and the wind swirled around the tree. The Crow drew in his wings and continued to explain.

"It is the wellspring of all dreams and where they come to die, God of Souls. Older than either of us can fathom, and once my sanctuary. Until Ulerne stripped me of my powers." A hiss escaped his beak. "After that day the Dream World closed to me. Now I am back." The Crow tilted his head with a short laugh. "Back in control. Take a step, God of Souls, if you dare."

Rafe hesitated, but risked it all. He moved one step towards the Crow. As his body moved, the surrounding tangibility altered, a barren world becoming blue sky over a beach.

"I should have known. Always the sea with you." The bird flapped a wing and the scene became a night-filled island under stars. "All the dreams of all the realms sail along the rivers of this world, tucked in between gods, mortals and Death herself. It is infinite as long as one creature breathes and dreams, and will only end when existence itself crumbles. This is where I learned who I am, what I am. This is where I first saw the stars." A sigh drifted into the illusion of night. "Someone, I don't even know who, dreamed their beauty here. Forever caught flowing through my world."

"Is this why you brought us here? In hopes I'll take pity on you? To persuade me to your side?"

"Would you be persuaded? I think not. And I need no one's pity!" The creature leapt into the air and the world changed; barren rock and bones surrounded them both. The Crow circled, faster than Rafe thought possible, and then dove at him. Rafe ducked on instinct more than skill. Even so, the Crow came within a hair's breadth of slashing Rafe with his claws. Kneeling, Rafe felt the substance of the world in his hand. He felt the connection with each and every realm. He smiled.

"That was a mistake, Crow." Rafe poured his magic into the very fabric of the Dream World, lighting it up in blue force.

"What are you doing?" the Crow screeched, caught in the crackling energy.

"Taking us far away from here."

In a flash of cascading radiance, they left the Dream World behind.

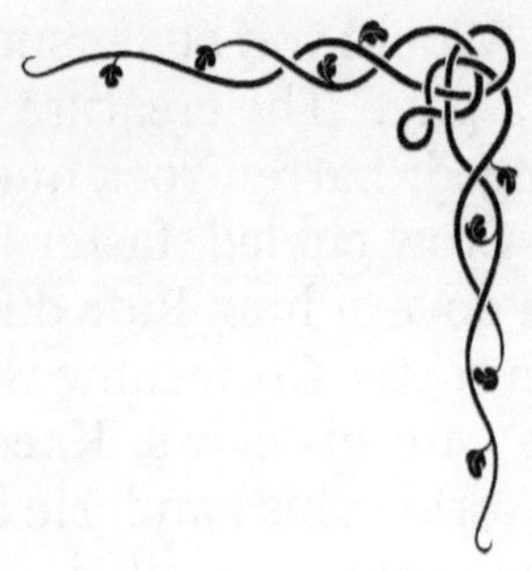

Chapter Twenty-Five
The Endgame Begins

They emerged in a world of darkness, streaked with faded light.

"Where are we?" The Crow flapped his wings and clacked his beak, settling down for a landing in the black mists.

"We're in the space between the After World and Death's domain. A limbo of shadows and twilight shade." Rafe grinned. "And far away from your dominion. I used your own realm against you, taking control of your Dream World to shift the pathways. One place became the other."

"Clever." The Crow bobbed his head, slight admiration in his tone. "Subverting the raw power to bring us here. You're learning to play the game."

"I've come to know your nature, little bird. Always with the tricks and traps."

The Crow spread his wings, stretching them to their full length. "Not so little, but you are right about my nature. But perhaps not so predictable as you think."

"Or more than you like to pretend."

"Perhaps." The Crow chuckled. "But you're the one who brought a Shadow Bird to the land of shadows." The creature flexed his wings and jumped, taking to the air in soaring flight. Swirling trails of black mist followed his path. Lost in the murky surroundings, the Crow soon disappeared from sight into the darkness.

Rafe watched him go with a smile. "There is no hiding here, Shadow Bird. This is my world."

He snapped his fingers and a tiny wisp of blue energy spun into the darkness, tracking the path of the Crow and following him. The bird flew deeper into the limbo between worlds, farther from the edge of the After World to skirt the boundary of Death's territory. Rafe stopped suddenly as the tiny wisp of blue remained still. He looked up, to see the Crow circling overhead, barely visible in the dark.

The bird cawed. "So predictable, so unprepared. Do you know what happens when death and dreams collide, God of Souls?"

A shiver ran up Rafe's spine as he replied, "No."

"Nightmares."

The Crow swooped down, fast as a cold winter wind, silver talons outstretched. Rafe dodged, throwing an arm out to defend himself, but a claw caught the back of his hand, cutting it.

"First blood to me!" The Crow laughed. "Just what I need. My plan still holds, in or out of the Dream World." He spat sparks of red magic from his beak, and from his claws he flung droplets of Rafe's blood into the air. "*Owed yndd ayg ofna.*"

Pain shot through Rafe's body and he fell to his knees. His heart thumped against his chest and his head pounded. His guts felt like razors sliced against his insides while his skin shivered in a frozen cold.

"What did you do?" His voice croaked and the words ripped pain through his throat.

The Crow settled to the ground in front of Rafe. "I told you, nightmares." The bird giggled, moving closer to Rafe. "When the real fun begins, you are mine." His talons gleamed a shiny silver in the blackness. "A helpless god is easy prey."

Rafe lowered his head as another wave of pain hit, but he also closed his fingers, and summoned his magic. Gritting his teeth past the agony, he blasted the Crow into the dark ether.

Squawking rage, the bird tumbled out of view, far away from Rafe, but shouted words floated back. "You're mine! The nightmares will find you."

And in that echo of the Crow's voice came a whisper. Indistinct, but harsh. Rafe lifted his head, watching grey mist form in the darkness. The air hissed and shifted and more manifest voices spoke.

"Arrogant. Pretender. Killer."

The mist formed shapes, faces of the drowned dead shifting in the haze. It moved, swarming around Rafe in a circle.

"Useless. You couldn't save us. Where were you? Why didn't you save us from the cold sea?"

The mist drifted closer and Rafe shivered. His skin grew pale, icy, and his breath shallow. He swung his head, staring at the visions, accusing eyes looking back.

"He couldn't save his sister from madness. Useless as a god. Useless as anything. An abomination to this world. His own family exiled him. Feared him. Who is he to have such power? What has he done worth anything?"

Each word stabbed at him, drawing on his own secret fears and pulling out the pain from his soul. He gasped, each breath an agony. He doubled over, his head dropping, his eyes half-closed.

"Tried to hide. Tried to run away. Coward."

Rafe shook under the weight of the accusations. Every thought he ever had of fleeing his duty flooded his mind. Every misgiving pressed on him, made his limbs heavy, his breath shallow.

"Not strong enough to be a god. Needed to make believe at being a mortal. Playing. Hiding. Run. Run. Run. Will doom us all. Doom his crew."

His mind screamed, replaying his failures, his lapses in judgement, everyone who died as a result of his inaction or mistakes. His weaknesses, real or imagined, hung on him like chains, dragging him down into a black despair.

"Give up. Give up. Let it go. Why bother? You do no real good in this world. Don't your efforts always make things worse? Think of the consequences. Black Axe Morgan, Manume, the Temple of Star Reef, Amaratha. All the people dead because you weren't good enough."

Against the fresh onslaught of uncertainty and blame, Rafe croaked, "No. Not my fault." Yet, in the back of his mind he didn't quite believe his words.

"Yes, it was. Not good enough. Not a god. Not a captain. Nothing. Nothing. Close your eyes. Stop fighting. Give in to your misery."

More pain knifed through him, and Rafe struggled against the magic, wrestling against the crushing need to sink into oblivion. He grimaced and forced words past his dry choking throat.

"No." He meant to shout but his voice only managed a whisper. "I won't give up. I won't give in to your twisting of my life."

For a moment, the voices stilled. Rafe heard a rustling beyond the mists. With an effort, he lifted his head.

A new voice sounded, deep and callous. "What a sad,

pitiful sight. Brought to your knees so quickly. But then, you never were much. Sailing around like a buffoon with such a hopeless crew. Pawns and converts following him, with no will of their own. Blind men following the fool."

Rafe curled his fist. One word left his lips. "No." A blinding flash of blue light burst across the void, dispelling the mist. Trembling, Rafe looked up. The Crow waited in the darkness. Rafe smiled as he collapsed.

The Crow walked over to Rafe's still form. He extended a claw, his low laugh breaking the silence. "Time to take what I need."

"It won't be that easy." Rafe's fist hit the chuckling Crow square on the side of the beak, spinning him onto his back, his feet waving in the air. "Using my own fears might have worked, if you hadn't thrown in your own insults and lies." Rafe staggered to his feet, breathing heavily, but magic surged through his veins. He loomed over the Crow. "And since you like dreams so much, let's see yours." In anger and frustration, Rafe tugged at the Crow's soul, shifting just enough of it to cast his deepest desire into the world.

Along the shadows of limbo, light unfolded, silver and serene, wandering among the stars. In a brilliance to make the heart leap in joy, the Realm of the Stars filled the void surrounding them. Then the images shifted, and in the flickering light, the image projected against the shadows showed the Gateway obelisk.

A tiny whimper escaped the Crow's beak. "So close, always so close." He turned his head towards Rafe. "All I want is to go home." The bird shook his feathers. "It's all I ever wanted since the starlight overflowed my vision."

Rafe sighed, resentment and anger mixed with pity. "I'm sorry."

"Please, please. All the power I stole, but never enough

to open the path. Even now, I still need your magic, God of Souls. I need you to unlock the gate." His wings flicked slightly, his voice turning to a pleading whine. "Help me. Combine your energies with mine and let me go." He cawed, a small entreaty echoing in the sound. "I'll fly to the stars and you'll never see me again."

Rafe gently shook his head, letting go his hold on the bird's soul. The images faded into nothing.

"No!" The Crow wailed. "Why do you all want to keep me here? You are all against me." Then he hissed and threatened, "If you won't help, then I'll fight you! I'll take what I need and leave your corpse to rot!"

Rafe shook his head again. "You can try, but even if you succeed, it won't matter. You cannot go back to the Realm of the Stars. I'm sorry. You don't belong there."

The Crow screeched. "I do belong! It's my home!" He struggled to his feet.

"No." Rafe stared, sympathy in his eyes. "As much as you wanted it to be, it was never your home. It was just a place you borrowed for a while. And you left behind your darkness, Crow. The stain cannot be allowed to fester there. Or grow. Your return would only destroy what you claim to love."

"Liar!" The Crow hopped a step and flailed his wings in a flurry of motion. "It was my home! I belonged! I don't care what you say, how you pretend, the stories you tell. I'll go home! I'll seize your power and you can be damned!"

Rafe gave a hint of a smile. "Do you truly think you can fight me and win? Even after this failure?"

The Nightmare Crow laughed and took to the air. He circled Rafe, still laughing. "Do you want to see who I am, God of Souls? Who I truly am?" He cawed loudly and deeply. "I may not have the power to open the Gateway, but I have enough to restore my former self! Behold the last Shadow Bird!"

The sky lit up in a blaze of crimson light and the Crow glowed a fiery red. His body convulsed and grew, his wings spreading, spreading, his body expanding. Suspended in the air, the form of the Nightmare Crow enlarged with snapping bone and swelling flesh, with feathers moulting in a shower of magic and decay, before they reformed along his body in a blackened cloak. His wings lengthened to six feet across, with a large curved silver claw jutting from each wingtip, their razor-sharp edges gleaming in the glow of magic. His height reached seven feet, his legs now long and spindly thin with splayed webbed feet that also sported silver claws. His beak elongated, becoming hooked, and as he opened his mouth, Rafe saw sharp, jagged teeth. The Crow, now Shadow Bird, tilted his head, red eyes glittering and a narrow tongue sliding from its beak. His wings flapped with a rush of air and he settled to the ground, glaring at Rafe.

"My true form. I am Dream Walker, Bringer of Nightmares. Shadow Bird." His long, full tail swished, amplified feathers slithering in the air and snapping like whips.

Rafe craned his neck, staring at the transformed avian monstrosity. He smiled, and the God of Souls enveloped himself in a sheen of shining blue energy.

"Impressive, Shadow Bird. It still won't be enough."

The two beings rushed each other, slamming great sparking bolts of energy at one another. Red and blue burst against each other and an eruption of light lit the darkness as the two magiks clashed.

Chapter Twenty-Six
The Return of the Shadow Bird

The void shook with the immense power shattering its structure, the aftershock reverberating through the After World and into Death's dominion. Light and energy stabbed through the shadows, slicing air and impermanence, cracking against the limbo realm and echoing across worlds.

Rafe and the newly formed Shadow Bird slammed together and apart across the in-between as their magic repeatedly sparred. They flew amongst the dark space, on wings and light, both whirlwinds of ethereal force, trading blows and flashes of energy in a vicious battle of wills and power.

As the combat heightened, the Crow screamed in joy, followed by a burst of laughter. "This is what I am! What I was born to be! What was denied me, God of Souls!" The edges of his wings lit in a radiance of scarlet, and swooped down slicing at Rafe, who barely dodged a lethal blow. The Shadow Bird circled around and dove for another blow, shouting, "I am the tempest! Only fit for the stars! You will not stand in the way of my freedom!"

Rafe summoned a shield of energy and took the full brunt of the blow while twisting into the momentum and smashing his full power back into his foe. The Shadow Bird flipped in mid-air and crashed beak first into the ground, with Rafe raining sizzles of blue magic into the creature.

"You are nothing!" Rafe snarled, letting every ounce of anger and resentment pour out of his mouth and into his magic. "A petty, selfish thing obsessed with a world that was never his. Obsessed with an illusion of what he wanted, who threw away everything he had to grasp artifice and ego!" Rafe summoned a bolt of energy, as fierce as any lightning, and stabbed the Shadow Bird.

The creature screamed, his body shuddering in spasms.

"Now to finish this." Rafe stepped back as the dazed Shadow Bird twitched, took a breath and summoned the dead from his mother's realm.

They rose from the blackness, from the depth of chaos and dread, swarming the Shadow Bird in seconds. Dozens of ghostly hands clutched at him, tearing at feathers, pulling at flesh and bone, dragging him across the void to imprison him in their grasp. He struggled and hissed but to no avail as spirits and phantoms held him down. When the bird lay supine, Rafe walked over, grabbed his beak, yanked his head back and put a foot on his throat.

"You took power that didn't belong to you, Shadow Bird. Time to return it."

Rafe's hand glowed blue and tendrils of magic snaked from his fingers, wriggling down and around the Shadow Bird's head and body. When the creature was securely bound by Rafe's power, the spirits let go and retreated back into the darkness. The Shadow Bird grappled with his restraints, red magic sparking in his eyes and along his wings and feathers, but he could not break free.

Rafe tightened his grip and whispered, *"Rwynd wynwer! Rwyncym rydyr hyndd yledus!"*

The Shadow Bird convulsed as red and orange veins of energy appeared across his body. Rafe flexed his fingers and drew the energy from the Shadow Bird into himself. The creature screamed as Rafe removed his power and his form shifted, shrinking until nothing of his former being remained, until only the Nightmare Crow lay at Rafe's feet.

The creature hissed and looked at Rafe, hatred and tears in his eyes. "Your grandfather would be proud. Victory is yours as is my power. Stolen back, as I stole it. How does that make you any better than me?"

Rafe let go of the Crow and took a step back, wisps of energy gently wafting around his fingers. "This isn't for me. I will use it to put right what you corrupted. Come and see."

Rafe waved a hand, the air glowing blue, and the world around them shifted again. Rafe and the Crow materialized inside the chamber room created by Reis.

"Your actions and the actions of Ulerne threw the realms out of balance. The magic you stole combined with your own essence," Rafe reached down and plucked a feather as the Crow screeched, "will restore the balance."

Rafe backed away from the Crow and released him from his bonds. The bird pulled in his wings and hobbled backwards, pressing against the chamber wall. Rafe moved to the centre of the chamber, keeping a watchful eye on the Crow, and gently tossed the feather in the air, along with a shower of magical sparks.

The aviary plume hovered there, black and sleek, suspended in the energy. Rafe inhaled and expelled the appropriated magic outward, showering it across the chamber, drawing it around the room in a circle. The columns vibrated, all three dancing in luminescence, in shades of red, blue and silver. The feather floated between them, shifting around the circle from pillar to pillar.

The trembling voice of the Crow asked, "What are you doing?"

"Chaos and Harmony used to be balanced. Three realms in each dominion. Until you and Ulerne collided and the Realm of Eternal Night was destroyed. The axis shifted after that day and now a new realm of Chaos must be created to restore the equilibrium. That is the first step."

"First step?" The Crow was curious now, despite everything.

Rafe nodded and flexed his fingers. The floor beneath his feet glowed and the stone showed images from the Realm of the Stars. The Crow gasped, desire and longing a thousandfold strong in the sound.

He whispered, "Home."

Rafe sighed. "And see what you've done to it." The thread of Chaos, the Crow's darkness, appeared in the images, snaking through the Light and the realm. "That is your legacy, Crow, to the place you profess to love. A taint, a stain, a corruption."

Rafe reached out, connecting to the dark magic, and snagged a thread of its shadow. He pulled it through the realms, bringing it into the chamber and melding it onto the Crow's feather. He gestured, making a circling motion with a finger and the feather slowly spun in the air, winding the thread in, twisting it from the Realm of the Stars back to its original source.

Once the thread began to spool along the spinning feather, Rafe blew a hint of magic in its direction and the plumage drifted to the column that glowed red, where it slowly sank into the stone. The pillar pulsed with dark energy until all the Crow's corruption drew itself back into the column.

"These stone pillars represent the realms. Harmony." Rafe gestured at the silver column. "The new Mortal Realm," he said, indicating the blue pillar. "And the Realm of Chaos." Rafe nodded at the last one, which now shimmered in red and black. "As it stands, everything is out of balance. Harmony holds three dominions, Chaos two, and the Mortal Realm stands alone. This is the harm you and Ulerne did, and what must be fixed." Rafe smiled. "Watch, little bird. The worlds are about to realign."

Rafe took a breath, closed his eyes and reached out with his senses. Deep within Chaos he felt the Crow's feather bound in the stolen magic and his link to it. On the other side of the circle he connected to the pulse of the Mortal Realm. He sailed along its eddies into the After World, and sent his essence beyond that into the land of Death, stabbing his power into his mother's world.

The Nightmare Crow flapped his wings and screeched. "What are you doing?"

"Putting things right."

The room exploded in a shimmer of brilliance, blue and silver, red and black, light pouring from every crevice and stone, every realm and void. The Crow screeched again but watched in fearful fascination.

And in the centre of it all, Rafe remade the worlds.

In a great grinding rumble, the column of the mortal world moved across the floor to occupy the centre of the circle as Rafe took a step backwards. The columns of Harmony and Chaos moved to opposite ends of the circle, making a straight row of stone pillars. Rafe heard the ricochet of prayers and fearful shouts as the worlds shifted, as the shockwave and unnerving echoes tumbled around the beings in the realms. All eyes looked upward, knowing not the source. Knowing nothing of a god altering destiny and their existence, only of the momentous occasion felt.

Satisfied with the positioning, Rafe moved to the last step. He reached deep within Chaos, holding tight the feather, and then yanked his mother's realm from the After World. It hovered, a speck in the void, before he bound it into Chaos with the primal magic of the Crow. The column shook with the sheer force of the transplanted world, but it held. Then Rafe let everything go.

In an instant, light, magic, colour all vanished, settling back to their new places in the order of things. The room stilled, suspended in an infinitesimal moment of creation and a newborn balance. Then a scream broke the quiet, a cry seething in ferocity and frustration.

"What have you done?"

The chamber filled with cold air and black mist. The Crow cowered against the wall, his wings folded over his head. Rafe merely turned around and smiled.

"Hello, Mother."

Chapter Twenty-Seven
The Shadow of Death

Death stood there, facing her son, a towering force in black, breathing frost and fury, as wisps of dark mist coiled around her and shards of sparking black magic radiated from her form. She glared a look that could kill a thousand mortals and repeated, "What have you done?"

Rafe repressed a chuckle. "I gave you what you wanted, just not quite the way you asked."

Behind him he heard a slight hint of laughter from the Crow. One glower from Death ended any amusement.

"I wanted my realm back!"

"That's what I gave you. A realm. Not the one you had, but something new to play with." Rafe moved forward and took his mother's hand. "I took the place you made in the After World and returned it back to Chaos. But with the Crow's stolen magic and his essence, I expanded it. There's a whole new realm for you, Mother, as large as the old one, ready for you to shape as you wish. Perhaps some of your old subjects from the Archipelago of Nightfall would even care to join you."

"How? Travel between realms, it can't happen without a gateway, and there's none in your world anymore."

"Then how are you here?" Rafe asked, grinning widely. "I made a few tweaks and rearranged a few barriers."

Death frowned, her shoulders shifting. "This is all very confusing."

"You'll get used to it."

"Wait, wait." A flurry of movement from the Crow drew their attention and the bird half-flew, half-hopped forward. "You opened gateways? Does this mean I can go back? Go back to the Realm of the Stars?"

Rafe looked down at the Crow, pity in his eyes. "No. I made sure no being of Chaos can ever cross into Harmony again, nor can Harmony cross into Chaos. Either one can travel to the Mortal Realm but not to each other. I set up new gateways, put barriers and restrictions into place that cannot be broken. Not by anyone."

The Crow stared and gave a heartbreaking wail. Rafe looked at him with pity, but Death...she looked at him with love.

She rushed to his side and knelt beside the Nightmare Crow, stroking his feathers as the bird cried his anguish to anyone or anything that would listen. "Shush, shush, my poor sweet one, it will be all right. It will be all right." She crooned a soft note of comfort and the Crow laid his head on her arm.

Rafe took a step towards them. "Mother, what are you doing? Get away from him!"

Death ignored her son, softly whispering to the Crow. "Come with me, come back and live in our new home."

Rafe gasped at her words. "Are you mad?"

Death glanced at Rafe with a smile, shaking her head. She turned back and caressed the Crow's wings. "Time to be a family again, my love. With me, with your brothers. With our son."

Death again looked up at Rafe, her last words carrying a realization that shuddered revulsion, but also understanding, through his blood. His stomach rolled, the taste of bile tickling the back of his throat. Rafe looked away, holding back the queasiness that threatened to overwhelm him.

Death ignored Rafe's reaction, returning her attention to the Crow. "Think of it. We can rebuild the world we had, together. It wasn't so bad, was it? You were happy there once before you saw the stars. We can start over. Reclaim that happiness."

The Crow moaned, a keening escaping his beak. He shook his body, ruffling his feathers and shifting his wings. He raised his head and looked at Death. "Do you mean it? After all I've done? After what I said earlier?"

Death nodded. "With all my heart."

"Good." A slight chuckle left his beak. "Then I still say *no!*" With a roar and a flash, using the last ounce of his magical energy, the Crow spread his wings, wrenching away from Death's grasp as Rafe moved to stop him. The chamber exploded in luminescence. Rafe and Death shielded their eyes, caught in the energy flare. When the burst subsided, the Crow was gone.

◆

The Nightmare Crow huddled on the edge of the in-between, suspended in the inky black void of nothing that defined the pathways holding the realms together and apart. He stared into the darkness, his breathing shallow, his feathers drooping, barely enough power to stay hidden, and not strong enough to flee into the Dream World. He had lost and he knew it. Yet, the stars still consumed him.

A whimper escaped his throat. "I'll get back. I won't

give up. Barriers or no, I'll return. Even if I have to tear apart his precious Mortal Realm, rip open the fabric of the realms to enter. I'll see the stars again."

Then a tiny sliver of light danced on the edge of his vision. The Crow gasped, unexpected hope rising in his chest. He raised his head, watching as a soft white light illuminated the darkness. The Crow spread out his wings, ready to fly towards the light. "Who's there? Ulerne? Don't hide from me. Have you come to take me home?"

"Oh, silly little bird. Still pining for the stars. Thinking you can win." A familiar feminine voice drifted from the shadows and two figures, Bevire and Manume, stepped into view against the pale backdrop of radiance. "Did you think you could hide from us? She who controls the dark, and she who lights the night? Silly bird."

"If he did, he's a fool. No one's hiding anymore!" Bevire softly chuckled.

"True, sister. The endgame came, but it did not belong to the Crow."

"It's not over!" The Nightmare Crow shuffled his feet, trying to stand, his wings fluttering. "I'm not done yet. I will not lose!"

"Oh, Shadow Bird. You already have." From behind the two goddesses another figure emerged. Death. She held a cage made of shadows and moonlight and pieces of shell, strong enough to hold a Shadow Bird.

Death smiled at the Crow. "I had this made for you. I hoped you would change, or be destroyed by my son. But in my heart I knew. Passion and Chaos do not die easily. Only Ashetus ever managed to kill a Shadow Bird." She exhaled a tiny touch of sorrow. "And he awaits you in my new realm."

The Crow flapped his wings and screeched, "I won't go!" He tried to fly, only to fall on his beak. Still, he defied her. "I told you I won't go back."

"You have no choice. Not any longer." She sighed, and a touch of frost edged his wings. She opened the cage door and moved forward.

"I just wanted to go home. Why was that wrong?" The Crow shrank back as Death advanced a few steps beyond where her daughters stood. "Why was that so wrong? Why should I be punished?"

"The Realm of the Stars was never your home, Shadow Bird." Death shook her head. "You are born of darkness, as I am. It is just a lie you told yourself, and those stars a place where you hid from your true heart. No longer."

Behind her mother, Manume smiled and let her light, her purest of magic, shine. Bevire did the same with her shadows.

"Time to greet your fate, little bird."

Strands of moonlight and threads of night shot across the space wrapping around the Crow and binding him tight. Death walked to her old lover's side and lifted him into the air by the neck. "I gave you an offer of redemption. Twice. You refused. Now I give you a prison." She shoved the bird into the cage and locked the door. The moonlight and shadows dissipated and the Crow banged his wings against the bars, shrieking, "Let me out!"

Death replied, "No." She looked at her daughters and smiled. "Thank you."

Then the Nightmare Crow and Death vanished.

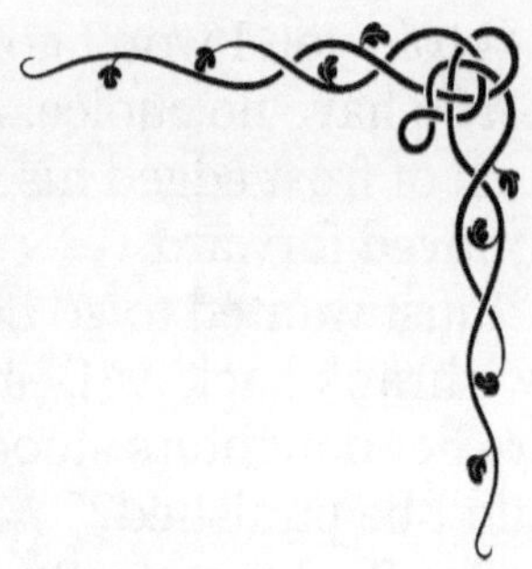

Chapter Twenty-Eight
Sunset Ending

Rafe and Reis stood in the temple courtyard, staring at the flickers of moonlight that lingered in the late afternoon air. Manume had come and gone, reporting of the Nightmare Crow's final fate.

"That's it then." Reis exhaled, his words full of relief. "It's over. After all these years."

"Not quite," Rafe remarked quietly and his father glanced at him with concern. "We need to put this island back where it belongs and free this place from the restraints you put on it. I unlocked the Gateway, and I think it might be more useful in the Archipelago of Nightfall."

Reis tilted his head, puzzlement creeping into his expression. "And why would that be? What are you planning? If you've realigned the realm pathways, why would it matter where the Gateway is located?"

"It will make it easier for some of the Archipelago's creatures to leave. I promised Mother I'd give them the option to join her in her new home."

"Oh." Reis became quiet for a moment. "I suppose some of them might be happier there. I know she would enjoy the company. She's been lonely. It's possible they may have been as well."

Rafe blinked. He had never even considered *that* possibility.

Reis smiled. "We'd best get to it then. I left the original catalyst stones buried here, so moving it back won't be difficult. If you can open a path, then I'll activate the spell and guide its return. I can inform the creatures of the Archipelago as well. They should remember and trust me well enough." He turned towards the temple before looking back. "Coming, son?"

Reis led the way into the temple and down the stairs that led to the catacombs. He did not lead Rafe there, however, and he instead turned to the right, veering off into another connected tunnel. They didn't walk far, only a few feet to a small, empty round alcove. Rafe noticed runes etched on the stone floor.

Reis moved around the room, flicking a drop of his magic onto each carved symbol. The air shimmered and, in the centre of the space, a large inky black stone appeared.

Reis glanced at Rafe and walked towards the rock. "A piece of the old realm and the keystone that is the centre of the translocation spell."

Rafe frowned slightly. "How does it work?"

"I placed six other stones at strategic points around the island and connected them to this activation stone. Once the spell is said, the magic will shift the island between realities and I can move it through the conduits to wherever in this world it needs to go. But I will need you to open the conduit. It's easier if I don't do both." Reis smiled. "Last time your mother did that bit."

Rafe nodded, absorbing the information. "Best not do

that here though. Opening a conduit would be safer out of the temple."

"Agreed. Once the spell is activated, I can control it from anywhere." Reis put his hands on the rock. "Step back. This won't take but a minute."

Reis took a breath and exhaled as his son moved back.

"*Gadwychyr unar. Ddrwys a rhywn. Tenithio adredd.*"

The alcove shook slightly and the stone vibrated, emanating a hum. Glowing silver threads snaked through its substance, marbling the surface in magic and light.

"There, it is done. The island is now in between realities, essentially vanished in its own temporary realm." Reis paused for a moment. "I do hope that won't alarm your crew. I never thought, perhaps we should have warned them."

Rafe smiled. "It might be a bit disconcerting, but they are used to strange happenings. I'll explain things later."

"Very well, shall we take this island home, then?"

Rafe nodded and they walked back upstairs and outside. There, both Rafe and Reis ascended on their magic to hover above the trees. Rafe reached out with his power and senses and opened a pathway large enough to send the island back to the Archipelago of Nightfall.

"There. Everything is ready. It will close once you reach the other side."

Reis grinned at his son. "Thank you. And after I'm done in the Archipelago, I'll return south and take steps to dismantle the Great Southern Mists. No need for that anymore, though it will take time to completely disappear."

Rafe nodded.

Reis reached into his pocket. "I do have one last gift for you. In case you'd like to do a bit of exploring." He pulled out his hand, concealing something. "Now that a certain map is unlocked, this will control it." He tossed Rafe a stone, shaped like a star and clear as glass. "Keep your mother's spells at bay." Reis winked.

"What?" Rafe sucked in a breath before turning the stone over in his fingers. "How do I use this?"

Reis chuckled. "I'm sure you'll figure it out." And in a burst of white light he vanished into the conduit, taking the island with him.

Rafe hovered in the sky alone, floating above the *Celestial Jewel.*

Rafe sat at his desk, the initial version of the map of the Lost Sea spread out in front of him, holding the stone his father gave him. "So how do you work, then?"

He tossed the stone in the air and caught it in the palm of his hand before grasping it between two fingers. He peered through its clear surface at the map, but saw nothing but the same image, distorted. He held it to the sunlight, rays dancing off its surface, and reflected the light over the map. Nothing happened. Then he placed the stone on the map itself.

The paper shimmered and the ink shifted. The gateway island disappeared from the map. Rafe inhaled sharply. Only the landmark of the Great Southern Mists remained and the strange runic markings. He nudged the stone across the paper, but nothing else changed.

"You are a stubborn one. Why won't you show me your secrets? You could at least show me one new island or landmass."

At his words the marking nearest the stone transformed to the shape of an island, and a name wrote itself on the map: *Spire Key.*

Rafe gave a low whistle and moved the stone beside another marking. "Reveal what this is." He paused, adding,

"And give me navigation bearings."

The ink swirled and the small depiction of a reef appeared with the name *Barbed Shoal* and navigational coordinates.

"Well, I'll be. So that's..." A knock on the door interrupted, and Rafe shouted, "Come in."

Blackthorne walked into the room. "Sorry to interrupt, sir, but the crew's wondering when we're heading out. Now that everything's done."

"Are they now?" Rafe looked down at the map. "We're fine with supplies, aren't we, Blackthorne? Enough for a month or two, correct?"

"Three months, sir. Is there a problem? We can sail home, can't we?"

"Oh, yes. We can sail home if we want." Rafe looked up at his first mate. "The question is, do we want? Do we head home, or maybe..." Rafe glanced at the map and back to Blackthorne. "We stay for a bit and explore the Lost Sea? I think there are islands here." Rafe grinned and tapped the stone. "I believe I've figured out this map. Mostly."

"Well, now, that changes things a bit." Blackthorne paused a moment before matching Rafe's grin. "It certainly would be a shame to waste such a thing, wouldn't it?"

"Indeed it would!" Rafe laughed and rolled up the map, putting both it and the stone in his pocket. He stood and walked around his desk. "Time to see Mr. Anders and set a course into the Lost Sea! We're going exploring."

Epilogue

The Realm of Eternal Night

In her reborn world, Death sat on her throne of bone and shadow staring into the sweet infinity of darkness she loved. By her right side rose an altar of stone where a birdcage rested, housing a morose and silent Crow. To her left stood a pole, rooted deep in the substance of the realm. Attached to the pole was a chain created from screams and teeth, ashes and tears, fastened to a collar around the neck of Black Axe Morgan. In the distance sounded the gurgles and splashes of a tentacled beast and the delighted cries of Shadow Birds as two uncles played with their nephew in a vast sea of despair.

Death let out a sigh of contentment. "Hear that, my pets? Our family is together again." She reached out and ruffled the feathers of the Crow through the bars of his cage. The bird clacked his beak and tried to move away from her touch.

"Cheer up, my love. Caged you may be, but at least your brothers visit you. Your son has even forgiven you." She withdrew her hand, adding, "One day I may even forgive you."

She turned to Morgan and yanked on his chain, pulling him within reach. Two more fingers were missing from his spectral form as was an eye. He shivered and moaned as Death ran a hand against his cheek. "Don't worry, my pet. I'm not in the mood for a bite of you today. You can keep your appendages for now. I'm not even going to torture you. I just want you to know. They're coming. And some of them may want to play with you." She dropped his chain and Morgan scurried back to his pole, trying to hide.

"Who is coming?" The voice of the Crow broke across the darkness.

Death turned in surprise, but answered. "The creatures of the Archipelago. Morrannan moved the Gateway back, let them know about this realm. Some of them are coming back to live here. Not all, but some."

The Crow clacked his beak again. "Why? Why would anyone return to this wretched place?"

Death laughed. "It's home, silly."

The Crow spat. "It's not my home! Never!"

Death laughed again. "Of course it is, Shadow Bird. For the rest of eternity."

The Crow turned his head away and closed his eyes. All he wanted was to sleep and dream. For in his dreams he still flew among the stars.

❖

The Realm of the Stars

For the first time in centuries Ulerne felt free. The burning radiance of his soul felt unshackled, the dark stain of burden, greed and ambition seared away. He wondered why such thoughts ever entered his mind, the memory of three Shadow Birds fading.

He looked around him and saw an empty throne room. No friends, no family. Only vacant halls. Puzzled, he called out, his voice rebounding through the realms. Many heard the invitation, yet only Reis came. Slowly, hesitantly, but he came. He walked back into his father's realm for the first time in centuries.

Ulerne smiled and held out his arms as if they had never been at odds. "Welcome home, son."

Reis embraced his father, and in an instant all was forgiven. All was right in both their worlds.

Pronunciation Guide

A partial list of name pronunciations.

Morrannan –Mor-an-in
Manume –Man-You-May
Lynna –Lin-Ah
Bevire –Bev-ear
Ulerne –Ool-earn
Reis –Ray-iss

Rafe's Family Tree

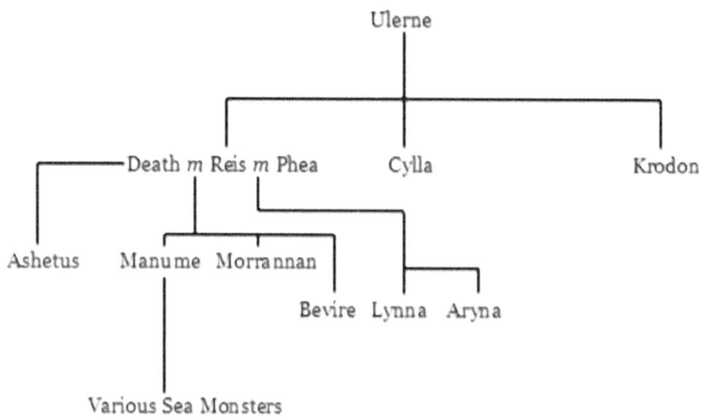

A quick peek at what awaits the *Celestial Jewel* in the Lost Sea.

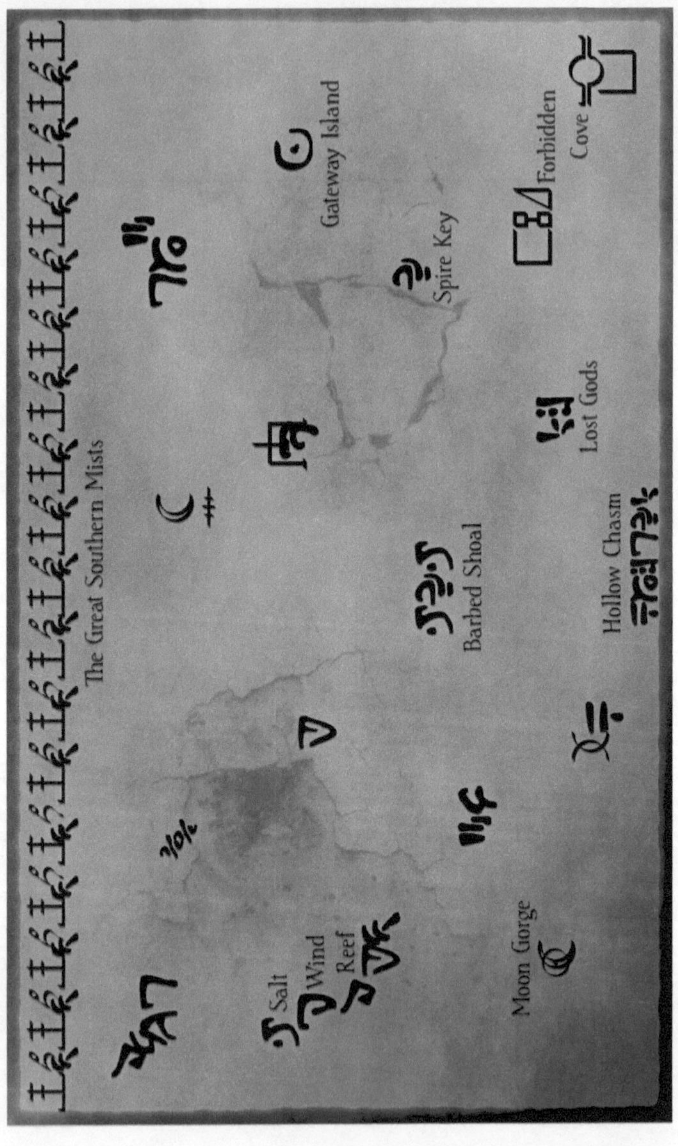

Also in the series

Ghosts of the Sea Moon
Souls of the Dark Sea

About the Author

A steadfast and proud sci-fi and fantasy geek, A. F. Stewart was born and raised in Nova Scotia, Canada and still calls it home. The youngest in a family of seven children, she always had an overly creative mind and an active imagination. She favours the dark and deadly when writing—her genres of choice being dark fantasy and horror—but she has been known to venture into the light on occasion. As an indie author she's published novellas and story collections, with a few side trips into poetry.